The Me[n] of
Roug[h]

Rory Mannion: Only county attorney Jessica Ingerson knows exactly how *old-fashioned* and macho this guy is. She finds herself wanting him and a future together. But Rory is on a mission to avenge a murder over a hundred years old, one that could still get him killed....

Clint Garvey: A typical cowboy—quiet and determined. Clint doesn't talk about the tragedies he's experienced, about losing the only woman he'd ever loved and being arrested for her murder. Everyone in Whiskey River knows about it and respects his privacy. Everyone except beautiful, impetuous Sunny. One day she just arrives at his house, claiming she's going to rescue him....
Ambushed, December 1996.

Gavin Thomas: As a writer, Gavin is able to imagine a lot of possibilities, but Tara Delaney catches him off guard. She pretends to be very straitlaced and proper, but he can sense a passion burning beneath. One he wants to untame.
Untamed, October 1996.

Three Real Western Heroes

Unforgettable

Author of over fifty novels, **JoAnn Ross** wrote
her first story—a romance about two star-crossed
mallard ducks—when she was just seven years
old. She sold her first romance novel in 1982
and now has over eight million copies of her
books in print. Her novels have been published in
twenty-seven countries, including Japan,
Hungary, Czech Republic and Turkey. JoAnn
married her high school sweetheart—twice—
and makes her home near Phoenix, Arizona.

Books by JoAnn Ross

HARLEQUIN TEMPTATION

537—NEVER A BRIDE (Bachelor Arms)
541—FOR RICHER OR POORER (Bachelor Arms)
545—THREE GROOMS AND A WEDDING (Bachelor Arms)
562—PRIVATE PASSIONS
585—THE OUTLAW
605—UNTAMED (Men of Whiskey River)

Don't miss any of our special offers. Write to us at the
following address for information on our newest releases.

Harlequin Reader Service
U.S.: 3010 Walden Ave., P.O. Box 1325, Buffalo, NY 14269
Canadian: P.O. Box 609, Fort Erie, **Ont. L2A 5X3**

JoAnn Ross
WANTED!

Harlequin Books

TORONTO • NEW YORK • LONDON
AMSTERDAM • PARIS • SYDNEY • HAMBURG
STOCKHOLM • ATHENS • TOKYO • MILAN
MADRID • WARSAW • BUDAPEST • AUCKLAND

ISBN 0-373-25709-0

WANTED!

This edition published by arrangement with Harlequin Books S.A.

® and TM are trademarks of the publisher. Trademarks indicated with
® are registered in the United States Patent and Trademark Office, the
Canadian Trade Marks Office and in other countries.

Printed in U.S.A.

Prologue

Whiskey River, Arizona Territory
1896

IT WAS THE smoke that first captured his attention. Hovering low on the horizon, the thick gray cloud was at odds with the blindingly bright day.

Rory Mannion muttered an oath and stiffened in his saddle, drawing a complaint from his bay mare, who tossed her black mane and sidestepped nervously. Having grown close to this man who'd rescued her from her brutal previous owner, she could sense his misgiving. And, more unsettling yet, his fear.

"Easy, Belle," he crooned, leaning forward to stroke her scarred auburn neck. "Everything's all right, sweetheart."

But his voice lacked conviction. Because deep in his gut, Rory knew better. He began galloping toward the smoke.

The ride took a mere ten minutes, but seemed an eternity, giving him time to think. He remembered, in vivid detail, how his bride had looked three days ago when he'd left her. Her thistledown blond hair, which she always wore in a tidy braid to bed, had been a golden cloud around her shoulders, which beneath her white muslin nightdress he knew to be as smooth and white as a field of new-fallen snow. But much, much warmer.

Although she'd tried to put on a brave front, her morning glory blue eyes had been bright with unshed tears and her voice had cracked as she'd begged him to be careful.

In an attempt to reassure her, he'd told her not to worry. "Your husband is a lot smarter than Jack Clayton. I promise he won't kill me."

Emilie's trembling lips had tried to hold a smile but she had shaken her head, unconvinced. She knew how evil Clayton was; her own father had been one of his innocent victims.

She'd told him jokingly that the next time she had him in a weakened condition, she would steal his shackles and manacle him to their four-poster bed to ensure that he'd never be able to leave her again.

Rory could understand why a new bride would want to keep her husband safely at home, but he also knew she understood that as marshall of Arizona Territory it was his job to bring the notorious hired gun to justice.

He'd bent his head and kissed her, a long, slow, deep kiss. He remembered how the scent of lilacs emanating from her fragrant flesh had filled his head, threatening to cloud his mind. How the soft little sounds she had made as she'd pressed against him so tightly the faintest breeze couldn't have come between them, had almost eroded his resolve.

As he'd reluctantly managed to put her a little away from him, the tears had overbrimmed her eyes, and for the first time in his life, Rory had felt like bawling himself.

He'd watched his bride of three weeks struggle for calm, uncomfortable with the depth of emotion that ripped at his heart. He loved Emilie Cartwright Mannion, worshiped her and could not imagine living without her. "I promise, I'll be back before you know it. Safe and sound."

And although he'd known he was playing with fire, he'd ducked his head one more time to give her a swift hot kiss, then before he could succumb to temptation, had released her and swung astride his mare.

Rory had not looked back. There'd been no need. Because the sight of his bride, standing there in her lacy virginal white nightdress, looking so forlorn and alone, tears streaming silently down her face, was frozen in his mind, like one of the photographs for which she and her father had garnered so much fame.

That three-day-old picture flashed before Rory's pained eyes again as he viewed his house—the cozy Cape Cod cottage he'd built for his homesick Boston-born bride-to-be, despite the fact that it looked so damn ridiculous here in Arizona—engulfed in flames fanned by the stiff high country wind.

Rory knew, with every fiber of his being, that the fire was Black Jack's doing.

"Emilie!" The raw anguish in his shout reverberated against the towering red rocks behind the cabin. Sunset stained the wide blue sky a bloody crimson.

An instant later the crack of a rifle shot echoed. When he felt the burning in his back, Rory cursed viciously. And as he slid bonelessly off the mare onto the hard ground, he vowed that Black Jack Clayton would pay for his crimes.

And somehow, whether in this life or the next, he was going to avenge his precious Emilie's brutal murder.

1

Whiskey River, Arizona
The Present

"I DON'T LIKE THIS." Sheriff Trace Callahan leaned back in his chair and eyed the woman seated across the desk with very real concern.

"I'm not exactly wild about it, myself," Jessica Ingersoll murmured. Her eyes and her voice remained absolutely calm, but knowing her well, Trace wasn't fooled. The quick swish of silk on silk as she crossed her legs for the third time in as many minutes revealed her nervousness.

"But there's nothing we can do," she reminded him. "According to a jury of his peers, Eric Chapmann is an innocent man. He's free to live wherever he wants."

"The guy's an amoral rapist who nearly killed some poor kid because she made the mistake of letting the small-town rodeo hotshot get her drunk. And then, when she threatens to turn him in, he burns down her house. I don't want the son of a bitch living in my town.

"As for anyone thinking he's an innocent man, as a prosecuting attorney, you know as well as I do that there's a helluva difference between being declared not guilty and being innocent."

"Granted," Jessica conceded. "Unfortunately, however we feel personally, the fact remains that I blew this case, so Chapmann goes free."

"You didn't blow it. That sleazy eastern lawyer Chapmann's daddy brought in to defend him was so good at smoke-and-mirrors tactics, the jury couldn't tell the difference between insignificant little details and rock solid evidence. You didn't stand a chance."

"I should have used more razzle-dazzle myself," Jessica said. She knew the verdict would still stick in her craw when she was a silver-haired old lady reduced to getting her daily courtroom fix by watching "Court TV" in the nursing home lounge. The case accusing the handsome young heir to a ranching dynasty of date rape, arson and attempted murder had garnered headlines all around the southwest.

Despite her best efforts, the jury had taken one look at the girl in question—a skinny, not very appealing waitress at Buster's Barbecue—and decided there was no way that a young man with everything going for him would have to resort to raping such a woman. After the trial, one juror—a grizzled old cowhand in his seventies—had stated that the girl ought to be damn grateful a good-looking, wealthy guy like Chapmann was even willing to take her to bed.

"You did great," Trace corrected. "It was the system that failed on this one, Jess. Not you."

"Thank you, Trace. I needed to hear that. Even if it was from a biased source." She sighed and smiled at him. Then crossed her legs again.

"And you're right. Monday morning quarterbacking never solved a thing." It also didn't erase the physical and emotional scars the young woman, who'd spent three painful months in a Phoenix burn center, would carry for the rest of her life.

"Too bad he didn't make a run for it when I went out to the Chapmann ranch to arrest the bastard," Trace muttered. "I could have just shot him and done everyone a favor."

"You wouldn't have killed a man in cold blood."

"No. But if I aimed right, I sure could have made certain he never raped a girl again." He paused, thinking about the rumors that had been running rampant since last week's verdict. "I was talking with Mariah last night," he began slowly, knowing ahead of time what Jessica's reaction would be.

"It's always nice for a husband and wife to be on speaking terms."

"She had a suggestion."

"Why doesn't that surprise me?"

"She's worried about you. As am I. So, we'd both like you to come stay at the ranch."

"I see." Jessica pretended to mull that one over. "I've always admired Mariah, but inviting your former lover to move in with the two of you is definitely proof that she's even more broad-minded than I'd thought."

"She knows I love her," Trace said simply.

"And she knows you didn't love me." Jessica had to smile at his distressed expression. "Relax, Callahan. What we had was great. But it wasn't the happily-ever-after, until-death-do-you-part kind of relationship you and Mariah are fortunate enough to share."

"I'm a lucky guy," he agreed, his eyes warming as he thought of his gorgeous, sexy, talented wife who was, at this moment, undoubtedly working away on her latest screenplay in her office just off their bedroom. That idea led to another. Perhaps, Trace decided, he'd go home early.

"Extremely lucky," Jessica agreed. "And please, thank Mariah for the offer, but I'm not going to let the two of you put me away in protective custody."

"The guy told people he was going to teach you a lesson," Trace reminded her.

She shrugged her silk-clad shoulders. "He's just another jailhouse braggart."

"He said the same thing to his lawyer." The hotshot attorney may have been a slime bucket, but he'd risked his license by breaching attorney-client privilege to warn Trace about the threats before returning to his cushy Manhattan penthouse law offices.

"Chapmann's a pathological liar," Jessica countered. "I wouldn't believe a single word the creep said."

"I do."

That flat, no-nonsense tone garnered her reluctant attention. "All right," she said with a frustrated huff of breath, "I'll admit that I'm a little concerned. But I'm not going to give him any power over my life, Trace. And as much as I truly appreciate the offer, moving in with you and Mariah would be doing exactly that."

His handsome face revealed his dissatisfaction. And his reluctant acceptance. "I told Mariah that's what you'd say."

"And?"

"Hell, she knew it, too. But she figured we ought to give it our best shot." He dragged his hand through his hair as he considered the unlikely friendship that had sprung up between the two women who both meant so much to him. "How about at least coming to dinner?"

"So Mariah can have a chance at changing my mind?"

"No. I promise, the subject won't come up."

"Ah, so now you're claiming control over your wife. Isn't that just like a man?" This time Jessica's laugh was rich and bold. It had once possessed the power to stir his blood. These days he was able to admire it on a purely objective basis. He also thought it was a damn shame it was wasted on him.

"You need to get married."

"What?" She crossed her legs again and stared at him. "Where in the world did that come from?"

"I don't know." Uncomfortable at having blurted out his thoughts, Trace shrugged. "It's just that you're a beautiful woman, Jess. And smart, and dedicated, and sexy as hell...." His voice drifted off as the devilish gleam that had suddenly come into her eyes reminded him exactly how sexy. "It just seems such a waste."

"Perhaps to you." She stood up and smoothed out nonexistent wrinkles in her forest green silk skirt. It was late in the afternoon, but she still looked as good as she had when she'd shown up for their breakfast meeting at the Branding Iron Café at seven-thirty that morning. Trace had often accused her of spraying herself with Teflon before leaving the house in the morning.

"But as I once told Mariah, I have no intention of getting married." She went around the desk and gave him a brief, friendly kiss on the cheek. "I much prefer the idea of being your kids' crotchety old-maid godmother."

That said, she waggled her fingers. "Good night, Trace. Give your lovely wife my love."

"What about dinner?"

"I've got a hot date."

"Oh?" He pretended uninterest even as he knew Mariah would be relentless in grilling him for details when he got home. "Anyone I know?"

Jessica grinned at him from the doorway. "Orville Redenbacher and Brad Pitt. I rented *Legends of the Fall* for the umpteenth time and plan to pig out on popcorn and lust after the fair-haired blue-eyed boy."

It was, she told herself as she drove home from the courthouse, a perfect evening. She might even open that bottle of champagne stashed away in the refrigerator. The one from the attorney general, anticipating her win in the Chapmann case.

That idea sent feelings of anger and frustration surging through her.

"No!" She slammed her hand down on the steering wheel. "This is your night for some long overdue pampering. You're not going to rehash old cases, or even think about work. You deserve this."

Pep talk over, and eager to begin her uncharacteristic night of indulgence, she stepped on the gas, risking a speeding ticket. As she neared her house, located on the outskirts of town, she saw something lying across the road. At first glance, she thought it was a coyote that had been a bit too slow in crossing the road, but after a longer second look she realized the prone shape was a man. She slammed her foot down on the brake pedal and at the same time twisted the steering wheel.

There was a screech of rubber on pavement, along with the acrid odor of smoke. Then the car shuddered to a sudden stop only inches from the man's outstretched arm.

Her heart pounding painfully against her chest, Jessica unfastened her seat belt and left the car like a shot.

He was, thank goodness, alive. She knelt down beside him and pressed her fingertips against his throat. His pulse was weak, which wasn't surprising considering the vast pool of blood he was lying in. The huge knot on his forehead was already turning a vivid magenta and blue. His eyes were closed, his lashes—so thick and curly they were wasted on a male, she thought fleetingly—rested on cheeks the unhealthy hue of ashes.

Her well-trained, logical, lawyer's mind clicked in, and her eyes swept the area for evidence as she ran back to her car to dial 911. Then she returned to the unconscious man and held him in her arms, not minding the blood that was staining her jacket and skirt as she murmured words of encouragement.

"It'll be okay," she said over and over again. "You'll be okay."

Although the ambulance arrived within six minutes, the wait seemed an eternity. Trace, who'd been on his way home, arrived just as the paramedics were transferring their unconscious patient into a helicopter.

Jessica explained how she'd nearly hit him. "If it had been just ten minutes later, it would have been dark enough that I might have run right over him."

"Lucky for him you didn't."

She frowned as she looked down at the pool of blood that was soaking into the asphalt. "Considering the shape the guy's in, I wouldn't exactly call him lucky. Did the paramedics tell you he was wearing a gun?"

"Yeah." Trace nodded. "One of them said it looked like one of those replicas of the old Colt peacemaker they sell at the gun shows."

She thought about that. "Perhaps he was taking part in some sort of reenactment?"

"I'm going to have J.D. check out the clubs and resorts in the county and see if any of them put on a Wild West show today."

"Good idea." The helicopter took off, the violent wind from the rotors whipping her tawny hair across her face. Jessica watched as the red running lights winked away. "I assume you're going to the Medical Center in Flagstaff to question him."

"That's the plan."

"I want to go with you."

He looked down at her with surprise. "I thought you had a hot date." His own hot date with his wife, Trace thought with resignation, would have to wait.

"Brad's going to have to wait. I nearly killed a man, Trace." Her hazel eyes were as serious as he'd ever seen them. "I want to know—need to know—that he'll be all right."

Trace shrugged, knowing the futility of arguing with her.

"You want to drive your own car? Or ride along with me?"

Jessica thought how typical it was that he was offering to drive. Although Mariah had raised his consciousness level considerably concerning male-female relationships, she had the feeling that deep down, where it mattered, Trace would always be just enough of a chauvinist to feel it his duty to protect the weaker sex. Namely women. That was one of the many reasons she'd never considered marrying him.

"I'll be fine. Really," she insisted with a frustrated laugh as he gave her a disbelieving look.

She was not surprised when he walked her back to her car and made sure that she fastened her seat belt before he returned to his Suburban. As she followed him down the nearly deserted Lake Mary's Road to Flagstaff, fifty miles away, Jessica couldn't stop worrying about the man who had literally fallen into her life.

RORY COULD HEAR them talking. A man and a woman. His voice quiet and deep, hers equally as hushed, but throaty, with the distinct tones of the eastern sea-board.

Hope surged through him. He had no proof Emilie had actually been in the house when it had been set on fire. Perhaps she'd escaped, after all.

"Trace," the woman said, "did you see that?"

"What?"

"He smiled."

"You're imagining things, Jess. The doc said he'd be out like a light for hours."

"He smiled. I saw it."

Jess. Not Emilie. But the determination he heard in those fluid feminine tones reminded him vividly of his bride. Who were these people?

"Hey, you." The female voice coaxed and at the same time her fingers skimmed over his forehead, brushing back his hair with a touch as soft as snowflakes. "You've slept long enough. Why don't you wake up and join the living?"

He wanted to. Lord, how he wanted that! If for no other reason than to get out of here, wherever he was, find out what had happened to Emilie and then, if nec-essary, kill Clayton.

But although he tried to raise his eyelids, he didn't have the strength. The last thing Rory felt, as he sur-rendered again to the darkness, was those incredibly delicate fingertips skimming so gently down the side of his face.

The woman was still there when Rory roused again much later.

"Oh, you're awake." Her voice was warm and pleased. He blinked, trying to focus on the face swimming in front of him. "We've been so worried."

We? he thought, but could not say. He blinked again, getting a blurry image of concerned hazel eyes. His vision became clearer and he noticed splotches of bloodstains darkening the front of her soft, unadorned shirtwaist. His blood? Rory wondered.

"I was shot," he remembered.

"That's what we need to talk about," a deep masculine voice said. Rory turned his head, then wished he hadn't when a lightning bolt shot through the top of his skull.

"Trace," the woman murmured, not bothering to hide her concern, "he's in pain."

"Then ring the nurse," the man suggested. "We've lost enough time as it is, Jess." He turned back to Rory. "I'm Trace Callahan. And you're—"

"Rory Mannion."

"As sheriff of Mogollon County, I have to ask you a few questions, Mr. Mannion. "

"Mogollon County?" Rory stared up at him, as confused by the reference as he was about everything else. "Where is Mogollon County?"

"It's in northern Arizona state," Jess offered. Rory could hear the encouragement in her voice.

"State?" His voice sounded rough, as if it hadn't been used for a long time. "Arizona hasn't achieved statehood. It's a territory."

There was a brief, significant silence as they stared down at him. "Do you know where you are?" the man professing to be a sheriff asked.

"Whiskey River, Arizona Territory." He stressed the word *territory*.

"And the date?"

"November 12, 1896." Emilie's birthday would have been next week, Rory thought miserably. The image of his house going up in flames shot through his pain and drug-fogged mind.

"I'm not certain how to tell you this," Trace said, "but you're a century off the mark."

"What?"

"But he has the date right," Jess added as she gave him a warm smile. "It *is* November 12."

Rory stared up at them disbelievingly. His mind whirled around and around, like an oak leaf caught in a whirlpool. When the effort to sort out the problem proved too difficult, he closed his eyes and drifted back into the void.

When Rory woke again, the room was draped in purple shadows. Night had fallen, as dark and as deep as a well. His head was throbbing; he felt as if he were nursing the worst hangover of his life.

"I'll call for the nurse," the now familiar female voice offered from the shadows as he rubbed his temple. "She'll give you something for the pain."

"No. I don't want any more drugs." He needed his head clear in order to think things through. To figure out what had happened to him. And more importantly, what had happened to Emilie.

"Well, aren't you the macho man." He detected both irritation and amusement in her tone. She stood up and came over to stand beside the bed and began massaging his temples. "You realize, of course, that you'll heal much faster if your body isn't having to fight all that pain."

Her tender touch was wonderfully soothing. "What pain?"

She sighed. "You're not exactly the most cooperative man I've ever nearly run over, and you're definitely the most stubborn."

She was wearing that same stained shirtwaist. It was indecorously open at the neck, which offered an enticing V-shaped view of her creamy neck. The material was thin enough that Rory could easily see her breasts rise and fall when she sighed. Although the drugs had nearly worn off, her spicy scent conspired with her caressing fingers to cloud his mind.

"You nearly ran over me?"

"On the road outside town. But I'm not the reason you probably feel you've gone ten rounds with Mike Tyson. Someone had already shot you before I showed up."

He had no idea who this Mike Tyson was. But he did recall when and how it had happened. "It was Jack Clayton."

Her fingers paused for a heartbeat, then continued their comforting strokes. "Are you sure?"

"Of course I am. He also burned down my house." The memory flashed through Rory's mind again, harsh and painful. "He's the only man in the territory mean enough to kill an innocent woman just to get to her husband."

Her fingers stilled again. "I think we need to back up a little. This Clayton killed a woman?"

"Not a woman." An icy fury swept over him, temporarily overriding the pain. "My wife."

There had been times, during the low spots of his life, when along with his revolver and his loyal bay mare, pride had been Rory's only possession. He was not a man accustomed to revealing weakness. But he'd be willing to beg, if that's what it took, to find out if Emilie had managed to escape the house.

"You have to find out what happened to her," he said. "I have to know if she died in that fire."

Poor man, Jessica thought, concern mingled with pity. He was obviously delusional. From the head injury? she wondered. Or had he been that way before someone had shot him and dumped him onto the road to die?

Trace had left over two hours ago. But he'd called from the historical society museum, where he had looked up November 12, 1896, in the archives.

This stranger had either been playing the part of Rory Mannion in one of the Wild West shoot-out shows put on for tourists, or he was a nutcase who truly believed that he was an old-time marshall, living a hundred years in the past. Whichever, he'd definitely researched his subject. Rory Mannion had indeed been shot to death—in the back—on November 12, 1896. The same day his wife had died.

"There was a fire," Jess said quietly.

"I told you that," Rory responded impatiently.

She nodded. Her hair, in the subdued light, gleamed copper, bronze and gold. Her eyes were sad. Rory hated the pity he saw in the hazel depths. "Emilie Mannion's body was found in the ashes."

Jessica decided, just in case he truly did believe he was Rory Mannion, not to mention that the woman had been trying to get out the door, which had been bolted from the outside. When Trace had filled her in on that unsavory detail, Jessica's blood had run cold, thinking of how terrified the young bride must have been. Since she possessed her own irrational fear of fire, the idea was even more horrific.

"I knew it." His voice sounded as if it were coming from far away and when he took his hands from his face, his eyes looked as if he'd just witnessed a glimpse of hell.

Then, as she watched, his square jaw firmed, his eyes cleared and a coldly determined expression appeared on his face. "I'm going after him."

When he tried to get out of the bed, Jessica immediately pushed him back down again. "You're not going anywhere," she insisted, surreptitiously pressing the call button on the side of the bed. "Doctor's orders."

A moment later, a woman dressed in white came bustling into the room. She had the wide shoulders and burly arms of a bull rider.

"Mr. Mannion needs something for his pain," Jessica said.

"I figured that's what you were ringing for."

Rory watched with concern as the nurse held up a small translucent cylinder with a lethal-looking needle on one end.

"Don't worry, honey." Before he could utter a word of complaint, the nurse had flipped him onto his side, and pulled up the ridiculous nightshirt they'd obviously put on him while he'd been unconscious. "You'll feel better real soon."

Although it took both women to hold him down, the hefty nurse managed to jab the needle into his buttocks.

"That should hold him until morning," she assured Jessica with satisfaction, as Rory fought against the soft clouds that were beginning to drift back over him.

Jessica continued to feel responsible for this man she'd literally picked up off the pavement, and didn't want to leave him. But after the nurse assured her he'd be asleep for some time, she went to the cafeteria for something to eat and a cup of coffee.

The only thing left at this late hour were some cellophane-wrapped sandwiches and gelatin squares that looked to be the consistency of Silly Putty and were an unappetizing shade of blood red.

She'd just sat down at one of the tables, and was unwrapping her turkey breast sandwich when one of the doctors approached from his own table across the room.

"Feel like company?" Dr. Kevin Green asked with a friendly smile.

As tired as she was, Jessica managed to smile back. She'd dated the orthopedic surgeon when she'd first arrived in Whiskey River and found him bright and interesting. The fact that he was also a control freak had her calling it quits after two months.

"Have a seat." The offer was unnecessary since he'd already sat down.

"The admitting clerk told me about your mystery man. Said something about him being dressed like an old-time sheriff."

"Actually, a marshall." The tin badge had been pinned to the shirt the emergency room crew had cut off him.

"Whatever." He shrugged uncaringly. "They also showed me his cool six-shooter."

"Trace says it looks like a very expensive replica."

"It's expensive, all right. But it's not a replica. It's a pearl-handled double action Colt .45. The same kind used by Wild Bill Hickok."

"Really?" She had grown up in Main Line Philadelphia, making her knowledge of western lore and traditions a bit sketchy, but even Jessica realized that if the revolver in question was a genuine antique, it would be worth a great deal of money.

"Really. Don't forget, collecting antique weapons is one of my passions. That gun is worth a very pretty penny."

"Then he's rich." Another clue, she thought.

"I'd imagine so." The beeper on his belt sounded. "Gotta run. I've got a patient in recovery. Another donorcycle accident." He frowned, then revealed that his true reason for coming over hadn't been for mere companionship. "Do me a favor and give the guy my card." He laid the discreet white pasteboard on the table between them. "In case he ever decides he wants to sell that sidearm."

"I'll do that." Jessica slipped the card into her purse. Her sandwich, which turned out to be as dry as it looked, went ignored as she sipped her coffee and wondered, yet again, exactly who was lying in that hospital bed.

2

RORY WAS TRAPPED in a world of heat and fire. He could hear Emilie's screams, but his boots were mired in quicksand and he was unable to reach her. Unable to save her as she reached out to him, pleading with her words and her remarkable morning glory eyes.

"I'm coming, sweetheart," he yelled out, trying to be heard over the roar of the wildfire winds. But he couldn't move. It was as if he'd been turned to stone. Fingers of flames were reaching out, flicking dangerously at her skirt.

Making matters worse was Black Jack Clayton, seated astride Rory's sweet bay mare Belle, laughing his fool head off. If the devil had a laugh, Rory thought miserably as the flames crackled and Emilie's cries intensified, it would sound like Clayton's.

The hem of her serge skirt had caught on fire. Black Jack pursed his lips, nearly hidden by the thick black mustache, and blew. There was a rush of wind and then a horrified Rory screamed as flames engulfed his bride.

He was drenched with sweat. And from the way he was tossing and turning, Jessica was afraid he was going to pull out his IV.

"He's not getting any better," she said worriedly to the nurse who'd come into the room to change bottles on the intravenous drip.

"He's not getting any worse, either."

"But it's been three days."

"We're doing all we can, Ms. Ingersoll." The faintly sharp edge to the nurse's tone revealed her irritation with a conversation they'd had innumerable times already. "Dr. Howard changed antibiotics last night. Hopefully the infection will respond to this new course of treatment."

Jessica could only hope so. Although she knew that Rory Mannion wasn't her problem, that she certainly hadn't been the one who'd shot him, then dumped him on the road and left him to die, she still felt responsible for him.

"Come on, Rory." She dipped the washcloth into the stainless steel basin of cool water, wrung it out and began moving it over his face again. His skin felt as if it were on fire. As she stroked the cooling cloth over his forehead, she was vaguely surprised it didn't sizzle. "You can beat this stupid bug."

Beneath his closed lids, the rapid eye movement revealed he was dreaming again. From his dark muttering and periodic shouts, she suspected the dreams were far from pleasant.

"Come on back," she coaxed as she moistened lips cracked with fever. "Believe me, it's a lot nicer here than wherever you are."

Although his flesh was flaming, he'd begun to shiver, as if he were suddenly freezing to death. It was not the first time this had happened, and as she continued, ineffectually she feared, to soothe him, Jessica had to fight the impulse to crawl into the narrow hospital bed, wrap her arms around Rory Mannion, and hold him tight until the violent tremors ceased.

Rory was in a tunnel, drawn to the glowing light. His pain was strangely gone, his mind calm. The soothing sense of peace and contentment that had settled over him was much like the feeling he always had after making love to Emilie, when they were lying together in the feather bed, basking in the pleasing afterglow of passion.

The light was growing brighter. And closer. Rory hurried, anxious to reach the source. As he ran out of the dark tunnel, he found himself on the banks of a crystal stream that flowed through a sun-brightened meadow ablaze with brilliant wildflowers. On the other side of the stream stood his bride, looking more beautiful than ever in that same lacy white muslin nightdress she'd been wearing when he'd ridden off to track down Black Jack.

"Thank God." The words came out on a rush of relieved air. Rory felt the cooling rush flow over him, like the clear blue waters flowing over the polished rocks at his feet. "I've been looking for you."

"I know." Her smile was as beautifully warm as always. Wanting her more than ever, needing her as he

*never had before, Rory tried to overlook the unchar-
acteristic sorrow in her wide blue eyes.*

"And now I've found you."

*And they'd be together, Rory told himself. For all
eternity. Just as they'd pledged on their wedding day.*

*Wanting to touch her, to hold her in his arms, to
cover those full sweet lips with kisses, Rory started to
cross the creek.*

*"I'm sorry, Rory, darling." She held up a hand.
Amazingly, Rory found himself frozen in place. "But
it's not your time."*

*"My time?" What the hell had happened to his legs?
"What do you mean?"*

*"I'm afraid we're going to have to be apart for a little
while longer."*

"No!"

*He'd already dreamed he'd lost her. Now that he'd
found her, safe and sound, Rory had no intention of
ever leaving her alone again. Let someone else be marshall. Let someone else right the wrongs and keep the
territory safe. Let someone else bring Jack Clayton in
for trial. Because from this day forward, all that mattered to Rory was his wife. And the children they would
have.*

*"It's a wonderful thought, darling," she said gently,
somehow seeming to read his mind. "And someday,
we'll have all that. But not now."*

*"Well, not right away," he agreed. They were both
young. They had years before they began a family.
Years they could spend loving each other.*

"Rory." She sighed and shook her head. "You're not making this easy."

Nothing had ever been easy for Rory Mannion. Except Emilie. From the first moment they'd met, Rory, who'd never believed in fate, had known they were destined to be together. Later, on their wedding night, Emilie had admitted to the same feelings.

"Making what easy?" The fear he'd felt during the nightmares returned, like icy fingers clenching his heart.

"You have to go back, darling."

"I'm not leaving you."

"You have to. For just a little while."

Her tone was as soft as ever, but unbearably firm. Unable to understand why his beloved Emilie was sending him away, Rory opened his mouth to argue further, when he was yanked backward, like a calf that had just been roped. And then he was being dragged through the pitch-black tunnel in the direction he'd come, away from the warm, comforting light. Away from his Emilie.

"Nooo!" he screamed.

He fought against the unseen force with every atom of his being, but his struggles proved fruitless. And then he was alone again. In the cold, cold dark.

A FAMILIAR SPICY scent, underlaid with a mysterious woodsy fragrance, was the first thing Rory noticed. He opened his eyes, blinking against the bright sun streaming in through the window, and looked over at a chair where a woman was sleeping.

Her clothing was absolutely indecent, he thought, taking in a soft wool shirtwaist that clung to the globes that rose and fell so seductively with her breathing. A pair of scandalously tight trousers covered her long slender legs.

When the sight of those long legs stirred erotic thoughts, Rory dragged his gaze upward to her face, which was framed by a sleek tawny fall of shoulder-length hair. Her full unpainted lips were parted slightly in an unconsciously seductive way that made him almost feel guilty for studying her while she was unaware and defenseless.

The sensual picture she made reminded him painfully of Emilie. It was just the sort of image she had delighted in capturing. While her father had achieved fame with his photographs of cavalry battlefield scenes and the brawny working men who were building the West, Emilie had concentrated her talents on depictions of everyday life. She'd begun taking photographs of women doing daily chores—washing, baking, bathing children.

That had led to photographs of women in the boudoir. Those unabashedly honest scenes of women in various states of dishabille, attending to their toilette, had won her a vast legion of admirers who compared her photographs to the art of Manet and Mary Cassatt.

Unfortunately, not everyone was enamored of those painters who'd been all the rage among art aficionados for the last decade. Indeed, Rory had first met the woman who would become his wife when he'd arrived at the Whiskey River opera house where several of her photographs were on display. A coalition of women representing the Whiskey River Morality League had filed a complaint, charging her with lewd and indecent conduct.

He'd studied the admittedly erotic photographs, but he hadn't found them lewd. Neither had he found their creator indecent.

On the contrary, she was delightful.

The first minute he'd seen her, standing in the middle of a circle of male admirers, Rory had felt as if his heart had stopped. When he'd heard her voice, he'd felt as if music had slipped beneath his skin. And when he'd looked down into those fathomless blue eyes, he'd known he was lost.

Rory groaned at the bleakness of a life without his Emilie.

The ragged sound roused Jessica. She rubbed the back of her neck which was stiff from her contorted sleeping position and unfolded her body from the chair which she was convinced had been designed by the Marquis de Sade.

"Finally." She stood up and smiled down at him. "Welcome back to the world of the living. Do you have any idea how worried I've been these past few days?"

The shadows beneath her eyes, suggesting a lack of sleep, backed up her words. She brushed his hair away from his forehead with a casual touch that was strangely familiar.

Their eyes met. And held. A flicker of distant recognition stirred in Rory, only to be banished by a harsh male voice.

"Dammit, Jess." Trace's voice, coming from the doorway, was edged with male aggravation. "Don't you ever go home?"

Since she'd been hearing the same complaint for days, Jessica didn't answer. "Our patient seems much better today," she announced.

"I'm glad to hear that." Trace's gaze flicked over her critically. "You, on the other hand, look like hell."

"Thank you. He's always been such a flatterer," she told Rory. Her hair, gleaming in the morning sunshine, reminded Rory of autumn leaves. But before he could think of the words to assure her that he found her lovely, the man took control of the conversation.

"In case you've forgotten, my name is Trace Callahan. Since you're obviously feeling better, I need to ask you a few more questions."

"First we need to call the doctor," Jessica said.

Trace frowned. "Jess . . ." he warned.

"You can question him later. Right now, he needs a doctor." That said, she left the room.

Trace cursed as he watched her go, then turned to Rory. "While we're waiting," he said, "we may as well get started, Mr. . . . ."

"Mannion," Rory answered, believing he'd already told the man his name. But perhaps he hadn't. The painful nightmares he'd suffered had melded so incomprehensibly with fact, Rory was no longer certain what was real and what was merely a product of his fevered mind. "Rory Mannion. I'm Arizona territorial marshall."

"Is that right?" Trace's tone remained absolutely agreeable, but Rory sensed that for some reason he didn't believe it.

Which didn't make any sense, since his accepting the job had made news throughout the territory. He hadn't been the first gunslinger to end up on the other side of the badge, but he had been one of the more famous. Or, infamous, he allowed, depending on your point of view.

Trace pulled a notebook and something Rory didn't recognize from his shirt pocket. "Mannion. That's with two Ns?"

"Yes." Rory spelled both his first and last names. He watched, fascinated by the strange, slender pen that appeared to hold its own ink supply.

"Are you the same Rory Mannion who killed three of the Gantry gang in that gunfight in Prescott?"

"Earl Gantry drew first," Rory said. "The others were set to ambush me."

"So I read." Trace's gaze, beneath the brim of his fawn Stetson, was shuttered as he looked down at Rory. "I hear you believe your wife has been murdered?"

Before he could answer, Jessica returned, the doctor in tow. All conversation ceased while the white-jacketed man pulled a cylinder from his pocket. It looked much like the one the sheriff had been writing with, but a light shone out of the end. After a brief examination, the doctor declared Rory basically sound.

"We'll keep you another twenty-four hours," he said briskly, "just to make sure you don't suffer a relapse. So long as your insurance coverage allows it, of course. Speaking of which, the clerk from records has some forms you need to sign."

With that incomprehensible statement, the doctor left the room.

Trace continued his questioning. "You were saying? About your wife?"

Although his tone was mild, Rory suddenly felt as if he were facing down the barrel of a Winchester rifle.

"I believe Jack Clayton killed her." He tried to keep his voice calm even as visions of that horror had his nerves screaming.

"I see."

The sheriff was beginning to irritate him. Didn't he have any feelings? Could he remain so cool, Rory wondered furiously, if he believed his own wife—or perhaps this woman named Jess, with whom he seemed to have a close relationship—had been murdered by a cold-blooded gunfighter?

"And Jack Clayton is . . . ?" Trace prompted.

Rory couldn't believe his ears. Since everyone in the territory knew who Black Jack Clayton was, he refused to even respond to such an asinine question.

"When I came back to town, our house was on fire," he said instead. "Clayton set that fire."

Trace exchanged another look with Jessica. "And that was November 12 . . . 1896."

"Yes."

"I'm afraid you're a little confused," Jessica said. Her voice was calm, but Rory could see the little seeds of worry in her eyes. "It isn't really 1896. It's 1996."

"That's impossible." Rory's first thought was that he was still trapped in the labyrinth of nightmares. But the room and these people certainly seemed real. Which could only mean that this sweet-smelling woman was some sort of confidence person. He began to sit up, cringing as the boulders tumbled around inside his head.

"Stay right there." Proving surprisingly strong for a slender female, Jessica took hold of his shoulders and pushed him down onto the bed. "I'll prove it."

As she crossed the room, despite all his problems, Rory found the movement of her hips in those tight denim pants more than a little enticing.

Oh yes, he thought, with bait like this to dangle before a receptive audience, he imagined the pair did very well indeed as they moved their scam from town to town. But what, he wondered, did they want from him?

She flicked a switch on the wall. The overhead light turned off. Another flick of the switch and the room was bright again.

"See? Electricity."

Rory was not overly impressed. "I first saw electricity at the Chicago World's Fair three years ago." He'd also seen Little Egypt dance the hootchy-kootchy, but decided that wasn't relevant to the discussion.

"Oh, I'm just getting started." She picked up a small black box from the table beside his bed, pointed it at a box on the wall and pressed a button.

"What the hell?" Rory stared at the scene flashing across the glass front of the box. He'd seen demonstrations of Edison's kinetoscope, but the films were nothing like this.

"Television." She flashed him a smile, then pressed a few more buttons, causing the scenes to change with dizzying speed. "One of the more dubious wonders of the twentieth century."

Rory's head, which had been throbbing when he'd awakened, felt on the verge of exploding as the visions flashed unceasingly before his eyes. As unnerving as the speed of the pictures was, the scenes they displayed of an unfamiliar world were even more frightening.

"I don't understand."

"It's obvious that you're experiencing some sort of mental disfunction from your head injury," she said in a sympathetic voice. "The doctor told us that was a possibility. He also said it would pass. In time."

Rory wanted to believe her. But he couldn't. It was too impossible. Yet, he wondered, how could he explain that picture box? And the furnishings and clothing, which now that he'd really begun to pay attention, he could see were different from those he was accustomed to.

An explanation flickered in the back of his mind. A few years ago a medicine show had come to Whiskey River. One of the highlights of the show—second in popularity only to the exotic, dark-eyed Gypsy dancer—had been a bearded Austrian mesmerist who'd entertained the crowd by putting various townspeople into a trance.

Although at the time Rory had believed the entire act to be a farce, he had to admit he'd enjoyed watching that stuffed-shirt banker, Harvey Bringle, crow like a rooster.

He also recalled watching Emma Lou Masterson hanging imaginary clothing on an invisible line. He'd suspected she truly believed she saw her husband's Levi's blowing in the breeze.

This was what was happening to him, Rory decided. For some reason, he'd been taken prisoner by a pair of skilled mesmerists. That had to explain all this. Because otherwise, he was insane.

He folded his arms across his chest. "I have nothing more to say. To either one of you."

"I don't get it," Trace grumbled five minutes later as he filled a large foam cup with coffee from the hospital cafeteria's stainless steel vat. "The guy freaking doesn't exist."

"Of course he does," Jessica replied mildly.

"He's not in the computer."

"A lot of people aren't in your precious computer," she said as she chose a smaller cup. The black coffee looked like something that could have leaked out of the tanker *Exxon Valdez*. Right down to the slick film on top.

"Not that many escape." He plucked two Danish from a tray, put them into the microwave oven and set it to warm for ten seconds. "Most people have a driver's license. Or a credit card. Hell, Rory Mannion doesn't even have a social security number."

"I don't believe they had social security cards back in 1896."

The microwave dinged. "Would you try to be serious?" He took the rolls out, cursing as he burned his thumb on the melted white frosting.

"I'm sorry. It's just that you're kinda cute when you're annoyed, Callahan."

"And you're annoying when you're being cute." He took her coffee out of her hand, put it on his tray and paid the cashier.

"So," she said as they sat down at a table in the corner of the room, "what do you think? Does he have amnesia, like the doctor suggested? Or is he delusional?"

"Frankly, I don't give a damn. That bullet hole in the guy's back isn't fantasy. Somebody wanted Mannion, or whatever the hell the guy's name is, dead," he reminded her. "And they almost succeeded.

"Meanwhile, there's a possibility we've got a missing wife, who may or may not have burned up when the shooter set Mannion's house—if he even owns a house—on fire. I need to find that gunman. And I need to find him yesterday."

"Have you tried boot hill?"

"Dammit—"

"I'm sorry." The laughter in her eyes said otherwise. She hadn't realized exactly how much emotional energy she'd invested in her mystery man until he'd turned the corner that morning. Although she figured she could probably sleep for a week, she definitely was feeling upbeat.

"But you have to admit it's certainly one of the more interesting crimes we've had lately." And far more mysterious than the Chapmann case, she thought.

"Did I ever mention that I hate mysteries?"

Jessica took a tentative sip of her coffee and was unsurprised when it tasted a lot like an oil slick, too. "I believe that came up. During the Swann investigation."

Trace frowned at the memory of Laura Swann Fletcher's murder. For a woman who was much beloved in Whiskey River, there had been a lot of people who'd had their own reasons for wanting her dead.

When he'd first arrived in the small mountain town from Dallas, Trace had been burned-out. Believing that the ability to care had been eaten out of him by the corrosive acid of experience, he'd planned to spend his days whittling toothpicks, waiting for his paycheck to arrive.

Then other lives had drifted down Whiskey River's currents, had drawn him into their midst and challenged his jaded outlook. The person who'd most changed his life was Mariah Swann. The woman who'd started out as a pain in the ass, had for a brief time been a suspect in her sister's death, and was now his wife.

"Perhaps the fingerprints you took will identify him," she suggested helpfully as she opened the blue packet of sweetener and dumped the contents into the too-bitter coffee.

"Do you have any idea how long it will take to get an answer back?" he complained. "It's not as if we're dealing with a homicide case here."

"No." She tried the coffee again. It was still undrinkable. "But it could have been if the gunman's aim had been a little more on the mark. And if our mystery man does have a wife who turns out to be dead, then it's a whole new ball game."

"True. But right now, all we've got is a head case with a bullet wound, which doesn't make us a high FBI priority."

He won Jessica's admiration by taking a deep swallow of his own unsweetened coffee. "And as much as I hate to burst your little bubble of contentment this morning, you realize, that if there really is a dead wife out there somewhere, your mystery man might be the killer."

"No. He's not."

Trace arched a dark brow. "You have no way of knowing that. Just because you've established some kind of weird bond with the guy while he's been unconscious for the past three days doesn't make him innocent."

Since she couldn't argue with that, Jessica didn't answer.

"I hate mysteries," Trace muttered again.

Jessica was about to suggest, as she had on numerous occasions, that if that was really true—which she knew it wasn't—he was in the wrong business, when a woman in a gray pantsuit came marching up to them.

"Sheriff Callahan," she said, slapping a manila folder down onto the table with a force that sent Jessica's coffee sloshing over the rim of the foam cup, "I want to know if the county is going to pay for that man you brought in the other night."

"I didn't bring him in," Trace said. "Technically, the paramedics did."

"You've certainly questioned him enough times. And Ms. Ingersoll has been spending all day and night in his room."

Jessica looked up from mopping at the liquid spreading across the tabletop.

"I wanted to make certain he didn't leave the hospital before Sheriff Callahan returned to question him again," she answered, not quite truthfully.

She was not prepared to try to explain her admittedly inexplicable feelings for Rory Mannion. She'd tried telling herself that having almost run him down, it was only logical that she'd care about his condition. She'd even attempted to convince herself that her only interest in him was professional. But she knew, deep down inside, neither of those reasons explained why she was so emotionally drawn to him.

"Well, if the county isn't going to pay the bill, who do I send it to?" the woman demanded.

"How about just giving it to the guy when he's released? Like you do every other patient," Jessica suggested.

The woman folded her arms across the front of her man-tailored suit. "And how would you suggest I do that?" she demanded. "When he's already left the hospital?"

"What?" Jessica and Trace answered in unison.

Trace stood up so fast his chair fell over. As he ran back to the room where they'd last questioned Rory Mannion, Jessica was close on his heels.

RORY STRUGGLED TO keep his mind on his goal as he trudged doggedly along the route he hoped would take him to his home on the outskirts of Whiskey River. Shiny horseless carriages whizzed by him, so fast he could hardly track their progress, but Rory knew that they were not real. They'd obviously been put in his mind while he'd been unconscious, and had somehow woven themselves into his hallucination.

It was cold for November. Wearing only his boots, jeans and underwear, along with the shirt he'd swiped from the cart outside his hospital room—it appeared someone had taken his shirt and duster—Rory felt chilled all the way to the bone.

Dark clouds the color of pig iron reached nearly to the ground, blocking out the sun and lowering the temperature by several degrees.

When those very same clouds opened up and began dumping water on him, like water out of a boot, Rory cursed. Then he hunched his shoulders and kept on walking.

Five minutes after leaving the hospital, Jessica spotted him. He was bent against the wind, and seemingly oblivious to the pouring rain. She shook her head as she pulled up alongside him and rolled down the window on the passenger side of the car.

"You realize, of course," she said calmly, refusing to let him know how relieved she was to have found him safe and sound, "you're going to catch pneumonia."

"This isn't real. It's a delusion you've put in my mind."

"I see." It was, she decided, one way to explain the inexplicable. "I don't suppose you'd be willing to get into the car and explain exactly how I achieved this wondrous mind-altering feat?"

"No." He didn't bother to give her so much as a glance as he kept walking.

A car sped past, horn blaring at her for blocking the right-hand lane. Jessica didn't blame the angry driver. What with the heavy rain, the mist and the lack of sun, the visibility was almost nil.

"You're going to get us killed," she said.

"I'm not going to die."

"You may believe you're invincible, but there's a bullet hole in your back that says otherwise."

"That was from Clayton. And I'm not going to die—or rest—until I get my revenge."

"Revenge is for vigilantes. If you really are a marshall, you undoubtedly took an oath to uphold the law." Since logic had failed, Jessica decided to go with the flow and play along with his delusion.

"Clayton will get a fair trial," Rory agreed. "Then I'll hang him."

Another car roared by. Then another. "Dammit, Mannion." She pulled off the road, then got out of her car. In her hurry to leave the hospital, she'd left her jacket behind, which left her as unprotected from the rain as he was.

"What are you doing?" he asked when she appeared beside him.

"What does it look like? If you insist on walking in the rain, I'm going to keep you company."

He slanted her a sideways glance. Water streamed down her face, plastering her hair to her head and drenching her clothes. "You're crazy."

"Ah. I thought I was merely a hallucination."

Rory thought about that for a moment. "You're not," he decided. "But everything else is." That was, Rory assured himself, the only answer.

"This rain sure doesn't feel like any hallucination."

"It is." Although the chill that had seeped into the very marrow of his bones said otherwise, Rory held his ground.

Another car sped by. Then another. And another. A fourth one tore through a dip in the road, engulfing Jessica in a muddy spray.

"Dammit!" She stepped in front of him, stopping his obdurate march. "Look at me!" she shouted, dragging her wet hair out of her eyes. "I'm soaked to the bone and I'll be lucky not to be wheezing my lungs out this time tomorrow with pneumonia.

"You can keep walking until doomsday, Rory Mannion, or whoever the hell you are. Or we can both die from exposure, which seems more likely the way the temperature is dropping. Or you can trust me enough to get back in my car and let me take you someplace safe."

"Safe?" He arched a brow. "Like your sheriff's jail?"

"No. Like my home."

The words were out of her mouth before she could stop them. Terrific. Her caseload, always heavy, had been piling up while she'd been spending her days and nights in the hospital. The last thing she needed was to play housemaid and nurse to a man with amnesia.

He stood there, staring down at her. In his whiskey brown eyes Jessica viewed his blatant distrust.

"You're playing with my mind," he insisted yet again. "This isn't real."

She ground her teeth and muttered a particularly frustrated curse that Rory didn't remember ever hear-

ing from a woman before. Not even from the whores at
The Road to Ruin.

"You want real?" she demanded. Her hands were
splayed on her hips as she glared up at him.

And then suddenly those slender hands were around
his neck and she'd risen up on her toes and her mouth
was pressing against his, making Rory forget he'd ever
been cold.

3

JESSICA'S TEMPER FLARED into a sizzling passion that surged from her lips into Rory's blood; desire curled, hot and insistent like a fist in his gut. Her kiss was hard and hot and over far too soon.

"Is that real enough for you?" she challenged, her hazel eyes shooting golden sparks up at him.

"It's a start." His eyes flickered to her mouth. "But I need more convincing."

Before she could respond, he hauled her against him, his strong fingers splayed on her hips, digging into her flesh beneath the wet denim. His mouth burned over hers, his tongue probing deep, his teeth biting at her lips.

As he moved her back and forth against him, teasing the hunger that pressed rigidly against the rough wet denim of his jeans, a sweet, piercing heat radiated outward from the pit of Jessica's stomach.

Oblivious to everything but the wild desire whipping at her blood, she thrust her hand in his thick, soft hair, fit her body even closer against his, and surrendered to that wicked, wonderful mouth that was consuming her. As the rain sluiced down their bodies, as his hot and hungry hands moved over her, Jessica began to burn from the inside out. She was amazed that so much fire and water hadn't turned them to steam.

The soft, desperate moans escaping her ravaged lips were the most provocative sound Rory had ever heard. His heart was hammering in his chest when a roar like a bull elk shattered the silence.

"What the hell?"

Jessica had been flying. Higher than she'd ever flown with a mere kiss. The strident sound sent her crashing immediately down to earth.

"It's an air horn."

Horrified at her public display, and wondering what on earth had possessed her to kiss the man in the first place, she tried to pull away, but Rory refused to release her.

"An air horn?"

"On a semi." She tilted her head back and looked up into his uncomprehending face, realizing that whatever the cause, he obviously still believed himself to be a man of the nineteenth century. "A truck." She shook her head when there was not an iota of recognition in his steady gaze. "Never mind."

Whatever it was, Rory realized that the mood had been shattered right along with the silence. His fingers curved into the top of her arms as he put her a little away from him, and treated her to a prolonged look.

"You're wet."

"So are you."

"True, but it looks better on you." Before she could respond to his easy compliment, his gaze turned serious. "Am I insane?"

Her expression softened. A sheen of moisture brightened her eyes. She reached up and pressed her palm against his cheek and felt a muscle clench.

"Of course you're not," she soothed. "You're just confused. From the head injury."

"I am confused," he admitted reluctantly.

"I know. But perhaps, together, we can sort everything out. Once we get out of this rain."

The touch of her hand on his face was more than a little familiar. "You stayed with me," he remembered. "During the fever. You kept talking to me. You assured me that I'd be all right. That I'd live. You kept calling me back."

He hadn't wanted to come back, he remembered. He'd wanted to stay in the sun-spangled meadow with Emilie. But then Emilie had sent him away. And he'd vowed, while being pulled through that cold dark place, that he'd never rest until he made Jack Clayton pay for his crimes.

That was what Emilie had been trying to tell him, Rory decided now. That before they could be together, he had to kill the man who had murdered her and her father.

So. He understood his mission. But where did this woman fit into the plan? He gave her a long look, trying to understand.

"Why did you stay by my bedside?"

"I felt responsible for you." That was the truth. Not the entire truth, but all that she could understand.

"But you didn't shoot me."

"Of course I didn't. But I found you."

Finders, keepers. The old childhood saying flashed through her mind and Jessica wondered, although she knew it was an outrageous thought, what would happen if, having found Rory Mannion, she kept him all to herself.

She'd never, in her entire life, experienced such a mind-blinding reaction to a mere kiss. And although she knew it was dangerous to allow her mind to go off in that direction, such passion was definitely seductive.

"Why did you kiss me?" he asked.

Once again they seemed to be on exactly the same wavelength. Jessica laughed, a short humorless sound that revealed her tangled nerves and her own confusion.

"I have no idea. I was furious with you, and well, it just felt right at the time."

Like the touch of her hand on his face. Although his heart would always belong to Emilie, Rory knew he was in trouble when he found himself imagining how that soft hand would feel on other parts of his body.

"Do you always kiss men you're furious with?"

He remembered, with vivid clarity, Emilie responding the same way during their first argument as a married couple. Much, much later, after they'd made love, she'd confessed that she felt overmatched trying to argue with a man trained in the law, so she'd used the only method she could think of to shut him up. Her tactics had worked perfectly. Not only had he stopped arguing, her passion had burned the reason for the foolish argument out of his mind.

"No." Jessica still couldn't believe she'd responded so uncharacteristically. "You were the first."

Rory thought about that for a moment and decided he liked the idea.

"You're wet," he said again, closing his mind to thoughts he was better off not considering. "We should get out of the rain."

"Good idea."

"You know, if you turn out to be telling the truth," he said slowly, "I suppose this place is preferable to where I'd planned to end up."

She smiled, beginning to relax. It was going to be all right, Jessica told herself. He'd get his memory back, Trace would solve his crime, and she'd be able to return to the courtroom and win her case.

That's all she needed, she told herself. One good solid win under her belt. And then the world would be back on an even keel.

"Where's that?" she asked.

Rory did not return her smile. His eyes were as bleak and dark as a graveyard at midnight. And as lonely.

"Hell."

The frightening thing was, she believed him.

They walked side by side, not touching, but close enough to match their strides easily. She opened the passenger door, gesturing for him to get in.

Rory paused a moment, gave the car a long look, then climbed into the seat. Jessica closed the door behind him, then walked around and climbed into the driver's seat.

"What kind of automobile is this?" he asked, glancing around with interest.

"A Jag. A Jaguar," she elaborated at his blank look.

The name was fitting, Rory decided. The sleek vehicle looked as if it were made to go fast, like the jungle cat it was named for. It also made him wonder again if perhaps she was telling him the truth. Although it made no sense, perhaps he had somehow traveled through time, like the character in the H. G. Wells novel, *The Time Machine*.

Of course, he thought, perhaps the fact that he'd read the popular novel was why he was able to concoct this fanciful scenario in the first place. Perhaps he was still unconscious and dreaming this. The conundrum made his head ache.

"How does it go?" he asked, looking at all the dials and gages that vaguely reminded him of the controls on a steam engine. "Does it use an internal combustion engine?"

"Yes." She gave him a long look. "Isn't it funny you should know that, when you still don't believe it's 1996."

"The Germans, Otto, Benz and Daimler, built gasoline-powered automobiles eleven years ago," he told her. "The Duryea brothers produced the first American one three years ago, and Henry Ford introduced a similar model this year."

He hadn't seen it personally, but he'd talked to a man who'd been in Detroit when Ford had introduced his four-horsepower horseless carriage.

"There was also an automobile race last year in Chicago. . . . Don't you need me to crank start it for you?" It was a dirty, dangerous task, unsuitable for a woman.

"Thanks for the offer, but things have come a long way in the last century."

Rory watched as she turned a key in the metal column, causing the car to come to life with a throaty roar that once again made him think the Jaguar was well named.

A chime sounded. "You'll have to fasten your seat belt."

When he only looked at her, Jessica sighed and wondered how long this strange fugue state would last. If she had to explain every single little thing to him, she was going to be exhausted by lunchtime.

"Like this." As she leaned over him to pull at the strap, her breasts brushed against his chest and he experienced a twinge deep in his groin. The wet fabric of her shirtwaist clung to the luscious mounds and he watched their movement as she stuck the belt into the holder with a decisive click, then fastened her own.

"What's the purpose of this uncomfortable device?" he asked, dragging his mind back to more mundane matters. Thinking about this woman's breasts was far from prudent.

"It may be uncomfortable, but you'll feel differently about it if we crash and it keeps you from flying head-first into the nearest pine tree."

"Do you intend to crash?"

"Not today."

"That comes as a relief." His tone was as dry as hers.

Rory observed her carefully as she shifted the car into drive and stepped on the gas.

"You use a wheel to steer, rather than a lever?"

If this was a dream, it was the most detailed one he'd ever had. It crossed his mind that perhaps he should be writing all this down, for use when he woke up. If he could obtain patents on even half the things he'd witnessed thus far, he could definitely become a wealthy man.

Without taking her eyes off the road, she asked, "How long are you going to stick to this story about coming from the 1890s?"

"It's not a story. It's the truth."

"Right. And I'm Annie Oakley."

"You're far more lovely than Annie," Rory said. "Although she sure can shoot," he allowed. "Buffalo Bill's Wild West show came to Whiskey River last year, right before she retired. I never would have believed it if I hadn't seen it with my own eyes, but she shot a cigarette out of her husband's lips at thirty paces."

"Talk about your power of love," Jessica muttered. "I can't imagine trusting anyone enough to risk my life that way."

"That thought crossed my mind as well, when I saw her do it," Rory agreed. "But her husband, Frank Butler, didn't even flinch."

"Good thing. Since that would've been the end of the act." She paused, then lifted a hand off the steering wheel and struck her forehead. "Damn."

"What's wrong?"

"Now you've got me doing it."

"Doing what?"

"Talking about Annie Oakley and Buffalo Bill as if they just came to town yesterday."

"It was last year," he reminded her.

Jessica's only response to that was a muttered curse.

The pain was coming back with a vengeance, making Rory disinclined to argue any further. He decided he'd think of some way to prove his claim later, when it didn't feel as if someone were banging away with a sledgehammer in his head.

He settled back into the comfortable glove-soft leather seat, felt the warm air blowing on him and decided if Black Jack had actually succeeded in killing him, which had somehow caused him to end up in the next century, traveling had definitely improved in a hundred years.

That thought was driven out by the unpalatable idea that incredibly, he was about to die again.

"Do you always drive at this speed?"

Rory straightened his legs to brace for the impending collision. Now he understood the belt wrapped across his body; obviously, without restraint, if she had a sudden inclination to stop, they'd both go flying through the front window glass.

"Not always." Jessica frowned as she came up on a trio of slower moving vehicles. "I hate motor homes." Flooring the accelerator, she pulled out to pass. "On days like today, when it's raining, I try to go slower."

"You've no idea what a comfort that is."

As he viewed the huge horseless wagon loaded with logs headed straight toward them, Rory was tempted to shut his eyes but decided that having already been ambushed and shot in the back, this time he intended to face death head-on.

Just when he was certain his heart was going to break through the wall of his chest, Jessica managed to make it past the third vehicle and slip back into her own lane, seconds before the load of logs thundered past.

"You're a very reckless woman," he said when he could talk again.

"Do you think so?" She glanced over at him. "I've always thought of myself as being unrelentingly prudent."

"You?" Despite the circumstances, Rory laughed. "Since I have known you, you've taken a strange man into your arms, never mind the fact that he was bleeding all over your clothing—"

"You remember that?" This was, Jessica thought, a start.

"I didn't when I first woke up. Later, I kept thinking you looked familiar, but I couldn't place you. But now that the drugs have worn off, I recall more about the incident."

"Trace will be so pleased to hear that."

He heard the satisfaction in her voice and wondered about the relationship between his rescuer and Whiskey River's sheriff.

"I owe you a debt of gratitude," he said. "For getting me medical care."

"That's no big deal." She shrugged. "Anyone would have called 911."

The term was unfamiliar, but Rory understood the meaning. "Perhaps," he said, not believing it for a minute. "But not many of them would remain by a stranger's bedside for so many days and nights."

"Obviously I have a subconscious Florence Nightingale complex I didn't know about," she said blithely, not wanting to discuss her behavior until she'd figured it out for herself.

"So," she said, returning the subject to its previous track as she passed another car as if it were standing still, "what else makes you think I have reckless tendencies?"

"The way you drive, for one thing."

"Better watch it," she warned. "Any cracks about women drivers and I'm putting you out in the rain. For the record, I've never, ever, had an accident."

"That's commendable." Also astonishing, Rory thought. "How about inviting a man with a bullet hole in his back to stay in your home?" He would, of course, never hurt her, but she had no way of knowing that.

"Oh, that." She shrugged. "I'm not worried. Besides, I have a gun."

"You do?" That came as a surprise. It also reminded him that he'd tried to talk Emilie into letting him teach her how to shoot the Winchester.

"My work as a prosecuting attorney takes me in some pretty rough places and needless to say, I'm not a criminal's favorite person. A gun tends to even the playing field."

It had not been an easy decision for her to make. She'd always been against violence, which was why she'd gone into criminal law in the first place. She enjoyed putting the bad guys away so they couldn't hurt innocent people. Besides, having earned a reputation as the fastest mouth in law school, she'd been convinced she could talk her way out of any problem that might arise.

She changed her mind after she'd been beaten up, outside the Philadelphia courthouse where she'd been working late one night, by a fifteen-year-old gang-banger with an adult-sized grudge against the system.

"I recently said much the same thing to someone," Rory said quietly. If Emilie had been armed, would she have been able to fend off Clayton?

Jessica watched the bleak expression move over his face in dark waves. "Recently, as in 1896."

"Yes."

His unwavering answer brought to mind a popular country song title—"That's My Story and I'm Sticking to It." But seeing the lingering pain in his eyes, she decided not to argue the date. "I assume we're talking about Emilie."

"Yes." He dragged both hands down his face.

Once again his grief seemed genuine. Which was, of course, impossible. Because that would mean that his story was also real and there was no way she was prepared to believe that this man was truly Rory Mannion, marshall of Arizona Territory in 1896.

She remained silent, watching out of the corner of her eye, as he straightened his spine. And, she guessed, his resolve.

"There was one more thing you did that was dangerously reckless," he said, "and that was—"

"Kissing you." Jessica had no answer for such uncharacteristic behavior. It had been an impulse, pure and simple.

"Yes." He turned slightly in the seat, his gaze serious. "Some men would not stop when offered such encouragement."

When Eric Chapmann immediately came to mind, Jessica involuntarily shuddered. "I know." Her own gaze was as sober as his. "But somehow, I knew you were safe."

He laughed at that, but the rough sound held not a hint of humor. "Now that's where you're wrong," he corrected her grimly. "Because I'm the most dangerous man you're ever going to meet."

Once again Jessica thought of Eric Chapmann. Remembered his boyish good looks, his friendly smile. And his deadly eyes. And then she thought of the threats toward her he'd allegedly made.

"That's where you're wrong."

Her flat tone did not invite comment. There was a story there, Rory thought. But up to his eyeballs in problems of his own, he didn't pursue it.

They ride in silence, each lost in thought, the only sounds the *swish swish swish* of the wiper blades across the windshield, the *ping* of raindrops on the metal roof and the hiss of tires on the wet road.

Nearly an hour had passed on the Jaguar's clock when they entered the town of Whiskey River. The main street looked familiar, Rory thought, but there were many changes. Jessica pulled up in front of a building he remembered being the home of the *Rim Rock Weekly Record* newspaper. Only now, the brown-and-yellow hand-painted sign pronounced it to be Otterbein's Drugstore.

"What are we doing here?"

"The doctor gave me two prescriptions to have filled for you," she said. "Antibiotics for the infection, and pain pills."

Although he had always held a secret contempt for opium users, the idea of medicine for his increasing pain came as a relief.

"Why don't you wait here? And I'll be right back."

A gentleman would go into the store with her, Rory reminded himself, even as the warmth of the car, the comfortable leather seat and the pain all conspired to encourage him to do as she suggested.

"There's no point in arguing," she said, as if reading his mind. "Besides, I've got you strapped in. By the time you figure out how to release that seat belt, I'll be back."

He watched her walk toward the store, enjoying the sight of her rear end in those tight jeans that were, in their way, as scandalous as that brief skirt she'd worn the other day.

The door swung open just as she reached for it. A man came out and reluctantly stopped when it appeared she wanted to talk with him. He was tall and lean, obviously a cowhand, Rory decided. His hair was shaggy, he hadn't shaved in a very long time, and his eyes were red rimmed and puffy, suggesting a tendency toward the bottle.

Jessica's smile was warm and friendly, although there was concern, the look Rory was growing accustomed to seeing in her eyes. She lifted her hand to the man's hollow cheek in a way that seemed as natural to her as breathing. Rory was surprised when the simple affectionate gesture sent a jolt of some dark and dangerous emotion surging through him.

He watched them exchange a few words. Or, rather, she talked and the man merely responded with what appeared to be a few curt monosyllables. The car window kept Rory from hearing the brief conversation. But as the man walked away, he watched Jessica's shoulders droop and realized that whoever the cowboy was, he was someone she cared about.

Rory was reminded of Patsy, a pretty redheaded whore at The Road to Ruin who was always rescuing stray kittens, bringing them home to the comfort of the whorehouse. A former Boston beauty from a good family, whose downfall had come at the hands of a fast-talking Bible salesman, she was the pickiest soiled dove in the territory.

And although she was also one of the most popular, she'd never, to his knowledge, allowed any male to spend the entire night in her bed. That privilege, she'd told more than one downcast cowboy, was reserved strictly for her furry friends.

If what he'd witnessed was any example, this woman named Jess was just as prone to picking up strays. The difference, Rory thought, was that Patsy was smart enough to stick to the four-footed kind.

Jessica disappeared into the store, and giving into his throbbing headache, Rory leaned his head back and closed his eyes. He was drifting in that netherworld between sleep and awareness when a sudden tingling, like the electricity before a thunderstorm, skimmed up his spine, across his neck and down his arms.

He jolted awake and looked out the window at the man headed toward him down the sidewalk. The swagger was definitely familiar.

As was the face beneath the brim of the black Stetson.

It was Black Jack!

Rory ripped at the belt that had him tied to the seat and finally freed himself. With a string of curses harsh enough to turn the air blue, he fumbled with the unfamiliar door handle, then he was out of the car in a flash.

4

"SAW YOU TALKING with Clint outside," Walter Otterbein said as he filled the prescriptions. "Now there's a man on a slippery slope if I ever did see one."

Knowing that the pharmacist was a genuinely caring man, and understanding that he wasn't just gossiping for entertainment's sake, Jessica answered, "He's had a rough year."

"That's for sure." He counted out the red capsules. "Losin' the woman you'd always loved, not to mention your unborn baby, would probably drive any man to drink."

Jessica nodded in silent agreement. Clint Garvey's drinking was no secret; all you had to do was to look at the man to read the pain etched all over his craggy dark face.

She and Trace may have been able to put Laura Swann's murderer behind bars. But the sad truth was that justice didn't cure a broken heart.

"I hear you found yourself a stranger outside of town," Walter said as he poured the pills into a brown plastic bottle and began typing up the label on his old black manual Remington.

"I nearly ran over him."

"Yep. That's what I heard." He looked up at her. "From these, I guess he's out of the hospital."

"Yes." Jessica braced herself for the next question, wondering how she was going to explain that she was taking the stranger home with her, when the door to the pharmacy opened and her blood turned to ice.

"Dammit all to hell," the pharmacist muttered, revealing he was not any more thrilled by the appearance of this latest customer than Jessica was.

"Well, well," Eric Chapmann drawled as he caught sight of Jessica standing at the counter, "I thought that was your Jag outside, Counselor."

His smile reminded her of a shark—cold and deadly. His blue eyes, which could twinkle on command, were rattlesnake flat.

Jessica wanted to ignore him. But not wanting to give this sociopath the pleasure of knowing he had the power to upset her, she had no choice but to respond. "Since I own the only Jaguar in town, that's a fairly safe assumption." Her voice was frost, her eyes as cool as the November morning.

"Saw a man sitting in the passenger seat." He leered at her. "You got a new beau, Counselor?"

The hell with game playing, Jessica decided. Obviously he knew he could get under her skin. That being the case, she decided to go with her first instinct and ignore him.

When she turned her back to him, he merely laughed and wandered off down a nearby aisle.

"That boy should be in prison," Walter muttered beneath his breath.

Jessica wondered how long it would take for her to stop thinking of Eric's acquittal as a personal failure. Forever, she decided reluctantly.

"Unfortunately, not everyone agrees with you."

"Unfortunately, there are a lot of people in the county dependent on the Chapmanns' goodwill," Walter countered. "I'm not one of them." He stuck the label onto the bottle and placed it with a similar one in a white paper bag. "There you go. All done."

And just in time, too. Jessica couldn't wait to get out of the pharmacy. Eric Chapmann's presence had cast a pall over the interior of the store. Along with a dark sense of evil that she knew she wasn't imagining.

She opened her wallet and was counting out the bills when he moved up beside her, and stood too close for comfort. "Don't forget these." He tossed a handful of red boxes of condoms onto the counter beside the bag. "Now that you've got yourself a new boyfriend, Jess—" his voice deepened on her name "—your sex life should be picking up."

His blue eyes, which Jessica had heard teenage girls swooning over, laughed with insulting innuendo. Jess was reminded of a quote he'd given to MacKenzie Reardon, editor of the *Rim Rock Record*, asserting that the only reason the county attorney was going after a guy who had an active sex life was because it was obvious she had none of her own.

Jessica cursed inwardly at how good this creep was at yanking her chain. "My sex life is none of your business."

"That could always change." He gave her the boyish grin that had worked wonders on the women on the jury. "You're a damn right fine-looking woman, Jess. And, despite our admittedly rocky past, I'm willing to overlook our differences." His gaze settled on her breasts in an openly suggestive way that made her feel dirty. At the same time he put his hand on her hip. "If you are."

He was truly disgusting! Before Jessica could come up with a sufficiently killing response, the door to the pharmacy burst open and Rory came charging in.

"Get your hand off her, Clayton."

"Clayton?" Eric arched a brow and laughed. "I'm afraid you've got me confused with someone else. My name's Chapmann. Ask anyone in town. My family's been part of Whiskey River forever."

"We both know who you are." Rory's hand instinctively went to where his holster should be. And, dammit, wasn't. "Now, if you know what's good for you, you'll let go of the lady."

Jessica had always believed in fighting her own battles. Under normal conditions, she would have leaped in to assure Rory that she could take care of Chapmann herself. But there was something about the flinty hardness of his gaze and his soft, but remarkably deadly voice that gave him a mysterious power that wiped the words from her mind.

To her further amazement, Eric didn't throw back one of the fast, smart-mouthed answers he'd become famous for during his trial. Instead, he was looking back at Rory with an unmasked hatred that gave her goose bumps.

She had no idea how long the standoff lasted. Time seemed to have stopped as the two men faced each other, reminding her of Wyatt Earp facing down Billy Clanton at Tombstone's O.K. Corral.

Finally, just when she thought her nerves were going to shatter, amazingly, Eric Chapmann backed down. "No point in trying to argue with a crazy man," he muttered. He turned his back on Rory and was almost to the door when he paused, and shot Jessica another cocky, sexy look over his shoulder.

"Don't forget that protection, sweetheart. After all, these are dangerous times. A woman can't be too careful," he reminded her silkily.

With that veiled threat he was gone.

Rory was about to go after him, when one look at Jessica stopped him in his tracks. "Are you all right?"

"Of course." She had to push the reassuring words past the lump of ice that seemed to have become lodged in her throat. "And as much as I appreciate your chivalrous gesture, I'm capable of handling Eric Chapmann by myself."

Rory had watched the color drain from her face and knew otherwise. "So Clayton's calling himself Chapmann these days?" he asked instead.

"That's his name," Walter Otterbein said. "And who's Clayton?"

"The son of a bitch who burned my wife alive. Then murdered me."

Jessica groaned inwardly as the pharmacist stared at Rory. Terrific. It was bad enough that he thought he was Rory Mannion. Now, he believed Eric Chapmann was Black Jack Clayton.

"We'd better go," she said. She put a hand on his arm and felt the muscles tense, like boulders beneath her fingertips.

"You don't believe me, do you?"

She could have lied. Perhaps she even should have lied. But she couldn't.

"I believe you believe it," she hedged.

He smiled at that, a faint sad smile that strangely made her feel like weeping. "I suppose that's all I can ask for. Right now."

Although Jessica still had no idea whether or not he'd really lost his wife, or whether the story was just an additional manifestation of his delusion, the bleak expression cutting harsh lines into his tanned face revealed that his pain was emotional as well as physical.

They left the store together, got back in the car and continued the drive to her house. As he leaned back in the seat and thought back on his encounter with Clayton in the pharmacy, Rory understood what Emilie had been trying to tell him.

As impossible as the idea had appeared when he'd read it in that novel last year, it seemed that he'd somehow managed to slip through some unseen door in time. And as brokenhearted as he still was about losing his beloved Emilie, Rory began to realize that there was justice in the world, after all. It may have taken a hundred years, but Black Jack Clayton was finally going to pay for his sins.

Then, after exacting his revenge, Rory would be free. Free to join Emilie for all eternity.

"What is Chapmann to you?"

Jessica realized Chapmann's sexual innuendo could have led Rory to the wrong conclusion. "He's not a former lover or anything, if that's what you're thinking."

"That thought never crossed my mind," he said honestly. "A woman like you would never get involved with such a man, whatever he's calling himself these days."

"It's not that big a deal," Jessica said with a shrug. Okay. That was a lie. But she just wasn't up to getting into the sordid story right now. "Eric Chapmann raped a young woman. When she threatened to call Trace, he beat her up, then set her apartment on fire.

"I was the prosecuting attorney at his trial. The jury let him off. End of story."

"I can believe he committed the crime." Rory remembered stories of whores who'd made the mistake of taking Black Jack to their beds.

More than one had ended up with broken bones; none had escaped without painful bruises. He'd also been infamous for setting fires. Including, Rory thought painfully, the one that had killed Emilie.

"And I'm sorry, for you and the young woman, that he wasn't convicted. But I do not believe that it's over."

It was the same thing Trace had told her. Unwilling to consider the possibility that Chapmann would live up to his threat, Jessica kept her gaze directed straight out the window.

"It's over," she repeated, as if her firm tone could make it true.

Rory watched the way her fingers tightened on the steering wheel and decided that to argue the point would only upset her further. Obviously, the thing to do would be to keep Clayton-Chapmann from harming this woman whose heart was obviously far softer and more open than she'd admit.

The thought of the unsavory man caused a pall to settle over them, and neither Rory nor Jessica felt like further conversation. There were many subjects they'd eventually have to discuss, Rory thought, things too complex to handle in a car speeding through the pouring rain.

There would be time enough to convince Rory that he was still delusional later, Jessica decided, after he'd had his medication. The pain pills were bound to make him sleep. This time when he woke up, perhaps he'd remember who he was. And who hated him enough to try to kill him.

"Does this town have a historical museum?"

"Of course."

"I'd like to go there. If you have time," he added, remembering that as a prosecuting attorney she undoubtedly had work to do.

She didn't. Not really. "You should be in bed."

"I will be. Soon," he promised. "But there's something I want you to see."

Jessica sighed and turned at the next corner. "All right."

If Whiskey River, Arizona, looked familiar to first-time visitors, it was because the town had served as a movie set on more than one occasion. Gene Autry, John Wayne and Clint Eastwood had all ridden horseback down Main Street. So had Doc Holliday and Wyatt Earp, but for some reason Jessica had never quite understood, the make-believe cowboys had bigger displays in the historical museum.

Edith Flynn, a flamboyant, comfortably padded woman in her midsixties, greeted them with friendly cheer. "Come on in and warm up," she said. "Looks like the two of you got caught in the rain." She glanced out at the water streaming down the windows of the museum. "Good weather for ducks. And Lord knows, we can sure use the moisture after last winter's drought."

Rory and Jessica both murmured a vague agreement.

"I'd like to see whatever information you might have on Rory Mannion or Jack Clayton," Rory said politely.

"Oh, we have tons. That's quite a dramatic story," she replied, bustling off to a shelf on the other side of the room. "I've always thought that Hollywood should make a movie about Rory and Emilie. They were so in love that, as tragic as their deaths were, I think it was better that they died so close together."

She shook her head, causing a few stray auburn hairs to escape the elaborate twist on the top of her still bright head. "I can't imagine either one of them living without the other."

"Neither can I," Rory said softly.

Edith put a stack of books in front of him. "There's a lot more on Black Jack," she said. "But of course, he was pretty notorious."

"Do you know how he died?" Jessica asked.

"No one seems to know that. He left town shortly after the murder of Marshall Mannion and his wife. Just flat disappeared, which was lucky for him, since there was a warrant out for him. Dead or alive."

"He was never seen again?" Rory looked up from leafing through a thick book.

"Not around these parts. I always figured he'd been killed and his body dumped in some mine shaft. As useful as he'd been for the ranchers, the man got too cocky for his own good and burned down one too many houses. I think if he'd shown his face in town, he would have been hanged before nightfall."

"I don't understand," Jessica said.

"Clayton was a hired gun for the ranchers," Rory told her. "He got his start as an army scout before he turned to selling firewater to the Indians, rustling cattle and robbing trains. Then, when Pinkerton's started zeroing in on him, he began working as a hired gun for all the ranchers who'd begun to feel more and more under siege by sodbusters streaming west in their prairie schooners.

"His job was to get rid of any settlers who were interfering with their open range grazing. Clayton and his pals burned out some homesteaders and almost got away with blaming it on a local who was half-Navajo."

"Wolfe Longwalker," Edith agreed. "He was a wonderful writer. We have several of his books here in the museum. They've recently been reprinted."

"I've read them." Rory didn't mention he'd read the original versions. "Longwalker's name was eventually cleared, but Clayton had powerful friends in high places and never served time for those murders."

"Which was one of the reasons the old marshall was replaced with Rory Mannion," Edith filled in for Jessica. "There was a lot of debate about whether Mannion was more gunfighter than lawman. He certainly sent more than his share of men to boot hill over the years, but no one could deny that whenever he arrived in a town, things settled down."

She began leafing through the pages of a thick leather-bound book. "Here's a picture of him."

Jessica stared at the old sepia photo, stunned into silence.

She was not the only one to notice the resemblance. Edith's gaze went from the photo to Rory and back to the photo again.

"Gracious," she said, "put a handlebar mustache on you, and you could be him, in the flesh."

Rory decided she'd never believe him if he told her that he'd shaved the mustache off after Emilie complained it tickled. "I suppose there's a faint similarity."

"Faint? Honey, you're a dead ringer," Edith argued.

Jessica was feeling a little light-headed. She didn't have to look up at Rory to know the man standing beside her, and the man in the photo were the same person. But that idea was impossible. Wasn't it?

"They say everyone has a double," she managed faintly.

Rory glanced down at her with concern. She was suddenly too pale. Obviously, the truth of his circumstances was beginning to sink in. He decided, while her mind was unwillingly open, to prove his point about Clayton.

"Do you have a photo of Clayton?"

"I believe—" Edith flipped forward a few pages "—yes, here it is." She turned the book, revealing the picture of a grim-faced man wearing a gunbelt over a black suit.

Ice skimmed up Jessica's spine, making her shudder. Although there was no outward resemblance, as with Rory Mannion, no one could mistake those mocking evil eyes. They were, she realized, the same eyes that had followed her around the courtroom during the trial. The same eyes that had leered at her in the pharmacy. They were Eric Chapmann's eyes.

She dragged her gaze from that photograph to another of a young woman. The caption beneath the picture identified her as Emilie Mannion.

"That's the woman he killed?"

"That's one of them," Edith said. "That picture was taken on her wedding day. She sure was a pretty little thing, wasn't she?"

"She was lovely." Although it made no more sense than anything else that had happened to her over the past days, Jessica felt a strange bond with the young woman. "What a terrible shame she had to die so young."

"It sure was that," Edith said.

"May I borrow this book?" she asked. "Just for a few days?"

"Well, we don't usually encourage lending things out," Edith said. "But, you're not exactly just anyone."

She was so in love, Jessica thought. *So happy. She'd been looking forward to this day for weeks. She'd been looking forward to this night even more.*

"Excuse me?" Jessica asked, when she realized Edith had been speaking to her.

"I said, you're not exactly just anyone. If you can't trust the county attorney, who can you trust?"

"Who, indeed?" Jessica murmured, feeling an eerie sense of disconnection when the older woman closed the book. "We'd better go," she said. Her voice, usually so strong and self-assured, was little more than a whisper.

"Yes." He flashed a warm smile Edith's way. "Thank you very much. You've been a remarkable help."

Edith looked as if she were about to melt on the spot. "Anytime," she said. "You're more than welcome here, Mr...."

"Just call me Rory."

"Like Marshall Mannion?"

"Yes." He exchanged a quick look with Jessica, who was looking a little stunned. "Quite a coincidence, isn't it?"

With that he put his arm around Jessica's waist and ushered her out of the museum, leaving Edith staring after them.

"Are you sure you're all right?" he asked when they were back in the car.

"What?"

"Are you all right? I'd offer to drive, but—"

"No." She shook her head and took a deep breath. "I'm fine. Really." She took another deep, calming breath. "Or I will be. In just a minute."

Rory didn't say anything. He just waited, watching with admiration as she literally pulled herself together. The sight was painfully familiar. He remembered Emilie doing the same thing when she'd first viewed her father's body in the undertaker's office.

Minutes later, Rory and Jessica pulled into the driveway of her home. After the past few days, Rory would have sworn that nothing could surprise him. But he was not at all prepared for what he saw through the slanting silver rain.

"It's a Cape Cod," he murmured, more to himself than to her.

"I know it doesn't really fit into its location," she admitted with a quick grin that banished the lingering gloom caused by the meeting with Clayton and the visit to the museum. "But I like it. I guess you can take the girl away from the seaboard, but you can't take the seaboard out of the girl."

"Emilie always said much the same thing. I built her a Cape Cod cottage." He decided against mentioning he'd built it on this very site. She'd undoubtedly never believe him. "I painted it blue."

"Blue was my second choice." Jessica found the coincidence, if it was even true, she reminded herself, more than a little unnerving. "With white shutters. Then, at the last minute I decided to go with the white and green."

"It was a very good choice." His head began to throb as he remembered the way Emilie had vacillated between the two colors. She'd finally decided white would be impractical in such a dusty country.

"Thank you. I think so." She reached up on the visor and pressed a red square on a small rectangular box. A few seconds later a large door on the side of the building opened.

"That's very clever."

"It's also handy for when it's raining," she agreed as she drove into the garage. The door shut behind them. "Of course we're already so wet, I guess it doesn't really matter today."

"It was worth it."

"What was worth it?"

He smiled at her. "Kissing you was definitely worth risking pneumonia."

Jessica considered that idea for a moment, recalled with vivid, aching detail the heated kiss and smiled back.

They entered the house through the kitchen. The tile counters were uncluttered and spotless, suggesting to Rory that she did not do a great deal of cooking. A vase of autumnal-hued asters in the center of the table was a welcoming sight.

"This is very nice," he said. "You're very neat."

He recalled, all too well, how Emilie's counters seemed to have a constant sprinkling of flour on them from bread baking. And how, whenever she'd lose track of time in her beloved darkroom, the dishes in the sink would pile up.

"I work long hours," Jessica snapped, a bit defensively, Rory thought. "I can't spend all afternoon slaving over a hot stove."

He arched a brow. "Did I say anything?"

"No." She tossed her purse onto one of the empty counters. "But it figures a man claiming to be from the nineteenth century would expect a female to cook."

"Actually, I was thinking that the flowers were very attractive," Rory said mildly.

"Oh." She looked a little embarrassed.

"I was also wondering if they were from a lover."

His fingers were idly playing with one of the starry asters but his eyes were on hers. His voice was every bit as soft as it had been in the drugstore, and like that other time, it vibrated with a dangerous intensity. But this danger, she realized, had nothing to do with murder.

"Not that it's any of your business," she said, "but I bought them myself." She refrained from mentioning that she'd purchased them on impulse in the hospital gift shop to give to him, then decided that the gesture was too personal.

"That surprises me."

"Why?"

He plucked a bronze flower from the bouquet and slid it into her hair. "You're what? Twenty-five? Twenty-six?"

The gesture was unreasonably intimate. Jessica backed up a few steps, but she did not take the flower from her hair. "I'm thirty."

"And still unmarried?" The idea was incredible. Rory would have thought a woman such as this would have suitors standing in line to propose marriage.

"This isn't the 1800s," she reminded him yet again. "Reaching the august age of thirty does not make me an old maid."

"Of course not." Fire flashed in Jessica's eyes, revealing the surprising passion he'd already tasted. And yearned to taste again. "It does make a man wonder, though," he mused aloud.

She watched his dark fingers rub his chin, remembered with excruciatingly vivid detail how they'd felt on her body and knew she was in deep deep trouble when she wanted to experience that hot pleasure again.

The silence strained between them, like an elastic cord pulled too tight. She lifted her chin challengingly. "Wonder what?" she snapped.

The toss of her head caused the aster to slip. "If men of this century have lost their sense of adventure." He reached forward to adjust the flower.

"I don't want you to touch me."

"Of course you do," Rory argued mildly, as he lowered his hands to his side. "The problem is that you don't want to want me to touch you."

For a man who didn't even remember his real name, and had no idea what century he was living in, he'd certainly hit uncomfortably close to the mark. "The doctor wanted to keep you under observation another day," she reminded him. "So, since you refused to stay in the hospital, I'd suggest we put you to bed. Alone," she tacked on when she realized how her suggestion could be taken.

Humor replaced need in his brown eyes. "Once again, I haven't said anything."

"You were thinking it."

Since he couldn't deny that, Rory didn't answer. He'd been aware of very little pain since he'd seen Jack Clayton at the pharmacy, but now his headache had returned with a vengeance. And his back felt as if it were on fire.

"I'm fine," he lied. "But if it'll ease your concerns, I'll agree to lie down."

His complexion had faded to the color of ashes and grooves had appeared on either side of his mouth. He was obviously in pain. It was just as obvious he had no intention of admitting it.

Jessica sighed. "Come on, macho man," she muttered, taking his arm. "Let's get you off your feet before you land facedown in my kitchen."

"Women swoon," he said, secretly grateful for her steadying hand. His aching head had begun to spin. "Men do not."

"Of course they don't. And instead of those pain pills I just paid twenty bucks for, perhaps I should just give you a bullet to chew on."

"You have a very sharp tongue," Rory observed.

"So I've been told. And if you don't like it—"

"I think I do," he interrupted her planned retort. "You're a great deal like my Emilie. She looks as soft as dandelion fluff, but she has a very strong spirit."

Strong enough to send him away, Rory thought grimly. "Or she had," he corrected, closing his eyes briefly as he thought of his beloved bride's death.

"Let's get you to bed," Jessica repeated gently.

His eyes, when he opened them again, looked as dark and as lonely as a tomb and his only response was a slow nod of assent.

5

HER BEDROOM WAS one of the most lushly romantic rooms Rory had seen outside of a whorehouse. But unlike The Road to Ruin, where the scarlet-and-gold color scheme had been designed to hit a man straight in the groin, these pastel hues slipped beneath a man's skin and into his mind.

Rory felt as if he were walking into a bower of spring blossoms. Pink primroses climbed up the cream silk wallpaper, a riot of roses bloomed on the quilt and matching lace-trimmed curtains, and hand-painted violets adorned the drawers of the pine chest.

A milk-glass vase atop the chest held a handful of dried wildflowers and gilt-framed botanical prints of lilacs and peonies hung on the wall over the chest.

"This is a magnificent bed."

"It was my great-great-grandmother's," Jessica said. "I had it shipped from Philadelphia when I moved here."

The mahogany four-poster bed gleamed with the lemon oil that generations of Jessica's ancestors had rubbed painstakingly into its surface. "Magnificent," he repeated, running his fingers over a detailed carving of a pineapple on the tall post.

The sight of his fingers stroking that dark red wood sent erotic thoughts spinning unbidden through Jessica's mind.

"Where will you sleep?" Rory asked, feeling uncomfortably adulterous as his rebellious mind conjured up a picture of the two of them lying together in this exquisite bed.

"There's a couch in my den. It's quite comfortable." She knew that from all the nights she'd worked late on the Chapmann case and had been too exhausted to drag herself upstairs to bed.

"I don't want to put you out."

"Don't be foolish. The only other alternative is for you to take the couch, and you're far too tall.... The bathroom's in here." She opened the adjoining doorway. "It takes a while for the hot water to get up here from the tank in the garage, but once it does you'll have plenty for your shower."

"Shower?"

She groaned inwardly. "I suppose you don't know what that is, either?" This was becoming more exhausting than the time she'd baby-sat her two-year-old niece whose every other word had been *why?*

"I saw a shower ring in the Montgomery Ward and Company catalog," he said helpfully. "It fitted over your neck while you stood in the tub."

"That's close." She demonstrated the shower and the tub, as well as the flush toilet, which he seemed to find even more impressive than her Jaguar.

"This is truly a remarkable century."

"I'm so glad you think so. I bought you a toothbrush, by the way. I'll bring it up when I come back with your pills."

She returned to the bedroom, pulled the comforter off the bed and was about to strip the sheets off as well when he caught her hand in his. "That's not necessary."

"You'll want clean sheets."

"You look tired." He frowned as he traced the purple shadows beneath her eyes with his fingertip. "Believe me, Jess, I have slept under some very primitive conditions and this is fine." He remembered every detail of the cave he'd slept in the night before he'd returned to find his home in flames.

Strangely, this time his touch soothed instead of excited her. It made Jessica want to curl up between those flower-sprigged sheets with him and sleep for a hundred years.

"Well, I really do have to get back to work," she said. "I hate to think how much paperwork has piled up while I've been at the hospital. If you're sure you don't mind—"

"I'm sure." His fingers trailed down her cheek, around the curve of her jaw. "You have already been more than kind and bringing me into your home will make even more work for you."

"I couldn't exactly put you out on the street."

"Why not?"

Good question, Jessica thought as she looked up at him. "I just couldn't treat anyone that way."

Even as she said the words, she knew they weren't true. In her work she was constantly meeting people whose lives were in turmoil and she'd never, not once, even considered bringing any of them home with her.

Rory didn't believe her for a minute. Although they'd both been avoiding the topic, it was obvious that there'd been a strange bond between them from the beginning.

"We're going to have to talk about it," he murmured as he stroked the pad of his thumb across her unpainted lips.

Jessica did not even try to pretend she didn't understand what he meant. She looked up into his fathomless eyes and felt as if she were drowning. "Not now."

"No." He managed a faint smile. "Not now."

"I'll go get your pills," she said.

She'd no sooner left the room when exhaustion hit him like a John L. Sullivan bare-knuckled fist in the solar plexus. He sank down onto the bed. The pillows, piled up at the head of the bed, carried the scent of her hair. He inhaled the faint fragrance, felt strangely comforted and fell immediately to sleep.

Jessica found him, lying on his side, his feet still on the floor, his arms wrapped around one of the pillows as if it were a woman. The deep lines etched in his face had smoothed, and his breathing was slow and regular, suggesting he was sleeping and not unconscious again.

"Hey, you." She nudged him in the shoulder. "Wake up."

His only response was a muffled groan.

She finally roused him enough to toss a couple of pills down his throat. She held the glass of water to his lips, and felt as if she'd achieved a major accomplishment when she got him to drink several swallows. But then, before she could get him onto his feet, he was gone again, out like a light.

Sighing, she dragged his boots and socks off, then went to work on his filthy jeans and the scrub shirt he'd obviously stolen from the hospital.

By the time she was down to his old-fashioned underwear, it occurred to her that he definitely believed in carrying the authenticity of his costume to extremes.

She debated stripping the gray wool drawers off him, then decided to leave well enough alone. Since he was too heavy to move, she simply covered him with the comforter.

She took a suit and pumps from her closet, some panty hose from the dresser, then went downstairs and changed into her work clothes. She wrote a brief note explaining she'd gone into her office and stuck it on the upstairs bathroom mirror, in case Rory woke up while she was gone, then left the house.

"TELL ME IT'S not true."

Jessica glanced up from her desk to see Trace standing in the doorway. In his Wrangler jeans, wedge-heeled boots, plaid shirt and Stetson, he almost could have stepped right out of the pages of that book she'd borrowed from the museum.

"It's not true."

"Dammit, Jess." He yanked off his hat and raked his hand through his hair. "This isn't any time to be cute. Walter Otterbein tells me that you took that Mannion guy home with you."

"Since Walter was still behind his counter when I left the pharmacy, he has no way of knowing that for sure."

"Now you're talking like a lawyer."

"I am a lawyer. And you're talking like a typical cop who doesn't trust anyone."

"I am a typical cop. And I've got the scars to show what happens when you let your guard down."

Jessica had seen the scars bisecting his torso from the open-heart surgery he'd undergone after he'd found himself on the wrong end of a street-sweeper automatic weapon during what was supposed to have been a routine homicide bust.

"Then when I stopped in for a sandwich, Iris told me that Margaret Dawtry had told her that you'd bought a bunch of men's clothes at the mercantile," he said.

Jessica realized she should have known better than to try to keep a secret in this town. "Goodness, you have managed to compile quite a case on me."

"I'm a detective."

"You were a detective. Now you're a sheriff. Whatever happened to your plan to sit on the jailhouse steps, whittling toothpicks and watching the world go by?"

"I believe you're talking about Mayberry. And that's not my style."

No. It wasn't.

"You are, without a doubt, the quintessential knight in shining armor, Callahan."

She'd told him that before, during the Swann investigation. At the time, he'd denied it. Just as he did now. "I'm no knight. It's just that I care about you, dammit."

"And I for you." She stood up, crossed the room, went up on her toes and brushed her lips against his cheek. "But you don't have to worry about Rory—"

"It's Rory now?"

Jessica sighed, realizing she should be more circumspect around a man who, before moving to Whiskey River, had the highest case closure rate in the Dallas Police Department.

She thought about suggesting that it was good to be on a first-name basis with a man who was currently sleeping in your bed, but knew the quip would only frustrate him more. "Until he remembers who he is, that name is as good as any."

"What if he doesn't remember? What if he's running some kind of scam? Hell, what if he's a psycho who's escaped from a prison for the criminally insane?"

"He's not insane."

"You're sure of that."

"I'd bet my life on it."

He gave her a long look. "You realize that may be exactly what you're doing."

"No." She'd never considered herself the least bit psychic, but her instincts had always been right on the money. "He may be confused, but he's not dangerous."

The back and forth motion of his jaw suggested Trace was grinding his teeth. His gunmetal gray eyes were as hard as bullets as they attempted to stare her down. But Jessica, who'd watched him use that technique to get perps to confess, was unaffected.

"It's going to be all right, Trace," she insisted. "I'll be all right."

Before he could answer, her phone rang. Saved by the bell, she thought as she scooped up the receiver. "Jessica Ingersoll, Mogollon County Attorney," she answered in a brisk professional voice. "Oh, hello."

"It's the attorney general," she said, covering the mouthpiece with her palm. "He's calling about the shooting of that DPS officer." Fortunately, the traffic stop that had resulted in gunfire had not been fatal because the highway patrolman had been wearing his new Kevlar vest.

"Yessir," she said as she swiveled her chair toward the window and away from Trace.

He muttered a curse, then left and headed back to his office to run Rory Mannion through the computer one more time.

IT WAS DUSK when Jessica returned home from work with a briefcase full of files, the museum book she still hadn't gotten a chance to look at and the shopping bags of men's clothing that had so irritated Trace.

She put the briefcase and her purse on the kitchen table, then went upstairs to check on her patient.

He'd obviously awakened at some time, at least long enough to strip off the underwear and crawl between the sheets. The pain pills must not have been entirely effective, she decided, noting the twisted bedding that suggested a great deal of tossing and turning. He'd kicked the top sheet aside, and although it still—just barely—covered the essentials, the sight of that long, dark leg with its rigidly defined muscles and tendons seemed vibrantly masculine when contrasted to the flower-sprigged cotton.

She tried to look away and failed. Tried to ignore the fluttering in her stomach and failed at that, too. Assuring herself that any woman would respond to the sight of a stunningly handsome naked man in her bed, Jessica took some of the new clothes out of one of the shopping bags, tossed them onto a nearby wing chair, then left the room, determined to get some work done before dinner.

She took a bottle of fumé blanc from the refrigerator, poured a glass and took it, along with her briefcase, into the den. She kicked off her shoes, put some Vince Gill on the CD player and settled down to read about the life and times of Rory Mannion.

She'd known from Trace's check that the man had, indeed, been a marshall in Arizona Territory. She also knew, from what the museum curator had said, that like so many men of that time, he was considered by some to be more gunslinger than lawman. What came as a major surprise was that he'd been an attorney. With a law degree from Harvard University!

She was frustrated when the article just breezed over that vital fact, concentrating instead on the number of men he'd been rumored to have killed and the tragic circumstances surrounding the death of his new bride. And although she still didn't believe the man upstairs was who he claimed to be, after reading about Emilie Mannion's horrifying murder, Jessica, who'd always considered the law a noble calling, a light of reason in a complex, dangerous world, could definitely understand a husband's need for revenge.

When Rory woke up, his headache was nearly gone. The pain in his back, while still bothersome, seemed to be easing up. His stomach growled. Rory decided the fact that he was actually hungry for the first time in days was a very good sign.

He showered, washing his hair with the shampoo that left his hair smelling faintly of herbs and spices. He brushed his teeth and his hair, looked around for a razor, but couldn't find one. Which was just as well, he decided. Since his hands were still a bit shaky, he could easily have slit his own throat.

He dressed in the new clothes he found lying on a chair in the bedroom. They fit as if they'd been tailor-made for his body, which didn't surprise him. Rory suspected that anything Jess did, she'd do perfectly.

Immersed in reading, Jessica didn't hear Rory come down the stairs, which allowed him to watch her undetected for a moment.

She was deep in the book she'd borrowed from the museum and as he studied her, Rory suddenly recalled how, when she'd seen the picture of Emilie, her eyes had softened with a light that was as compelling as it was familiar.

It couldn't be, he told himself.

But it was.

Jessica was jolted from her reading by a sudden aura of crackling electricity, like heat lightning flickering on the horizon before a thunderstorm. She looked up to see Rory standing in the doorway.

"Hello," he said.

She put the book down. Stop that! she told her lips, which had curved into a dopey grin. But they refused to cooperate and to tell the truth, Jessica couldn't blame them. He looked so good in that formfitting western-cut shirt and crisp blue jeans that any woman with blood stirring in her veins would want to drool. And the stubble on his face, which could have made him look like a lot of the felons she'd convicted, was undeniably sexy.

"I didn't mean to disturb you," he said.

"You're not." Now that was a lie. She put the book aside. "It's time I fixed some dinner anyway. I skipped lunch today and I'm starved. I'll bet you are, too."

"I could eat something," he said. Like a horse and a couple of steers for starters.

"I'm not surprised. They had you on a light diet in the hospital, but I never saw you actually eat a thing." She studied him more closely. "You look as if you feel better."

"I am, thanks. It's also nice to have clean clothes."

"I thought it might be. I bought them in town this afternoon."

Rory was glad they had not been left behind by a lover. "I'll want to pay you back." He'd been relieved to discover that Clayton had not taken the time to roll him after the shooting. Or else he'd missed the gold coins Rory had had in the pocket of his Levi's.

His expression assured Jess this was important. "Fine. Has your memory come back?"

He could lie, Rory supposed. But what was the point? "I know exactly who I am, if that's what you mean."

She exhaled a long breath. "You're still insisting you're Rory Mannion."

"I'd hoped you'd be more accepting of the idea. After seeing my photograph."

"A photograph that, granted, bore a startling resemblance to you. But that doesn't prove anything. I've been told that except for the difference in hair color, I look like Michelle Pfeiffer."

He gave her a blank look.

"She's a movie star." Another blank look had her throwing up her hands. "It's not important." She stood up, took her empty wineglass and started toward the kitchen.

For someone who professed not to cook, the aroma that wafted from the copper-bottomed pan was enough to start his mouth watering. "It smells very good," he said.

"It's minestrone. Soup," she said.

"I know it." He rubbed his unshaven chin. "But I thought you didn't cook."

"I don't. I picked it up at Mancuso's in town. I also got some lasagna and salad." She opened a foam container, stuck it in the microwave and pressed the timer.

Rory watched the meal spin around on the carousel. "Amazing," he murmured. He placed his hand against the black glass. "It's not warm. How does it work?"

"I'll tell you what," she suggested. "Tomorrow, if you're still having problems with your memory—"

"I have no problem with my memory." That wasn't exactly the truth. The problem was, he remembered too much. Rory thought the image of his house in flames would stick in his mind for several lifetimes. "You're the one who can't remember."

"Me?" She stopped in the act of pouring the tossed green salad into an earthenware bowl. "I have a near photographic memory."

"In this life, perhaps," he acknowledged obliquely.

She stared at him. "Are you suggesting . . . No." She shook her head. "You cannot possibly believe that I . . . that you and I . . . That's ridiculous."

He plucked a piece of red leaf lettuce from the bowl, dipped it into the container of oil-and-vinegar dressing, tasted it and found it delicious. "Fresh greens in

November," he murmured. "This is truly a remarkable century. And what, exactly, do you find ridiculous? The fact that you may have lived another life, in another time? Or the idea of you and I having been together in a past life?"

"I don't believe in past lives."

"Oh?" He angled his head, studying her with interest. "Why not?"

Good question. "I'm an intelligent woman."

"Only an intelligent woman could achieve your level of success in a male-dominated profession," he agreed easily. "But why does that preclude believing you may have lived before?"

"One of the reasons I chose law is because it's logical. At least most of the time," she amended, thinking about the Chapmann verdict. "There are legal precedents going back years, decades, even centuries, in some cases, which provide us with guidelines to follow—"

"Precedents like *prima facie*," he interjected quietly.

The Latin legal term meant, literally, on first appearance. "Exactly," she said. "How do you know that?"

"Since you were reading the book you borrowed from the museum, you should have read that Rory Mannion practiced law before accepting the job as marshall. And while *prima facie* evidence is admittedly common in the law, what we have here, Counselor, is a case of *sui generis*."

Of its own kind. Unique. Jessica knew all too well that the term was often used in legal decisions to indicate a singular set of events. Like time travel? No way.

She let out a short, harsh breath. "It's obvious that you have a nodding acquaintance with the law."

"I told you, I have a degree—"

"From Harvard. So, you want to tell me how a lawyer ended up a gunfighter?"

"It's a complicated story."

"Most of the good ones are."

She still didn't believe him. In truth, Rory didn't blame her. "I was in the army," he said. "I tried courtmartial cases. Then I got transferred out here during the time that the army was desperately trying to recapture Geronimo. I'd always believed what the government was calling the 'Indian problem' had nothing to do with me. When I started seeing some of the tactics the socalled good guys were using, I resigned my captain's commission and settled down in Prescott and set up a private law practice."

"The idea that you left the army suggests you weren't a proponent of violence."

"I wasn't."

"And I suppose you're going to tell me that someone forced you to kill all those men?"

"It's no excuse, but yes, in a way, that's what happened. I'd learned to shoot in the army, of course. And since Prescott wasn't exactly Boston, I carried a gun for my own protection. Much as you said you do," he reminded her.

"Touché," she murmured.

"Then one day, during a trial, my client's bank robbing cronies decided to try to help him escape. When they were going to shoot the judge, who was unarmed, I had no choice but to shoot them first."

"Them?"

"There were three of them."

"And one of you?"

"Who can explain why we have certain talents?" he asked with a sigh. "I didn't ask to have a good eye and a fast hand. It just happened."

"But you practiced."

"Of course. I had no choice, once the word got out and other men wanting to build a reputation or keep the unsavory one they'd already earned, started coming to town to challenge me. It was either them or me."

"From what I read, it was always them."

"It wasn't as if I went after them," he argued. "In the beginning, I'd try to talk them out of the fight, but it didn't take long before I realized that anyone crazy enough to want to go around killing people for sport wasn't about to be dissuaded. So, since I wanted to keep the frontier code of legal self-defense on my side, I made a rule of always letting the other fellow fire first."

"Wasn't that dangerous?"

He shrugged. "Not really. My opponent would usually be in a hurry to prove his point. That need to get off the first shot would make him miss."

"And you never did."

He sighed. "No. I never did. Which is why, I suspect, the people wanted me as marshall, to protect them from the criminal element in the territory."

"I read that one of the reasons for your popularity as marshall was that you treated everyone—white, black, Mexican, or Chinese, complainants or prisoners—exactly alike."

"The law doesn't make any distinction between races or classes," he reminded her. "At least, not ideally."

That thought brought her mind back to Chapmann.

"No," she agreed, knowing he was undoubtedly thinking of Clayton. "Dammit, you've got me doing it again."

"Doing what?"

"Discussing century-old events as if they'd really happened to you."

Rory closed the small gap between them and ran his palms over her shoulders. "I understand, all too well, how difficult it is to accept. But the fact is, no matter what logic you attempt to apply to this case, I truly am Rory Mannion and the last thing I remember is being shot by Black Jack Clayton in November of 1896.

"I also know that when I was caught in that netherworld between life and death, Emilie told me I must return to the physical world. I fought against leaving her, but she promised me we would be together again.

"And now, here I am, with you...."

"Surely you don't believe I'm Emilie?" Jessica stared up at him, terribly concerned about this latest delusion.

It was bad enough he believed himself to be a nineteenth-century lawyer turned gunslinger turned marshall. Or that he'd gotten the crazy idea that Eric Chapmann was his longtime nemesis Jack Clayton. But now, to believe that she was his beloved wife . . . Well, not only was that impossible, it could be dangerous.

What if he decided to force his conjugal rights? As weak as he was, she had no doubt that he was still much stronger than she. Dammit, Trace was right again, Jessica raged at herself inwardly. It had been dangerous bringing a virtual stranger into her home.

When she would have backed away, Rory's hands tightened on her shoulders. "You can't deny that there's been a connection between us from the beginning."

"It's chemistry."

"That, too." He lifted his hand and stroked her hair. "But there's something more important happening here, Jess. You know it—" he dipped his head "—and I know it." She watched, strangely hypnotized, as his mouth approached hers. "Like the way I know exactly how you're going to taste when I kiss you."

"That's not so surprising," she snapped back, struggling to regain control of the situation. "Since we've already kissed." A kiss she'd instigated. A kiss that had been a horrendous mistake.

"That was born of anger." His thumb brushed against her lips in a tender caress. "Which, while exciting in its own way, cannot equal a kiss that comes from the heart."

"Dammit, Rory—" She pressed both hands against his chest and pushed, but she might as well have been trying to move nearby Mount Humphries.

"You called me by my name." He exuded male satisfaction as he slipped a hand beneath her hair at the nape of her neck. "I've always liked the way you say my name, darlin'." His lips brushed against hers lightly, tantalizing, teasing.

His breath was like a summer zephyr, soft and warm. His stroking fingers threatened to lull her into compliance. Wondering if this was how Chapmann's victim had gotten herself into that almost deadly fix, Jessica fought valiantly against temptation.

"In this century, when women say no, men are legally required to listen."

"That's an admirable law." He began nibbling at her tight lips, encouraging them to soften. "But I haven't heard you say the word." His tilted his head, changed the angle ever so slightly and skimmed a ring of fire around her mouth with the tip of his tongue.

"Say no, Jess, straight out, like you mean it, and I'll stop right now." He kissed his way up her cheek. "But better yet," he suggested in a midnight-dark voice that wrapped her in velvet cords, "open your sweet mouth for me, and kiss me back."

She was in danger of melting into a puddle of need right in the middle of her kitchen. In the distance, over the wild pounding of her heart in her ears, she heard the bubbling of the soup on the stove, the *ding* of the microwave, the sound of the still-falling rain outside the darkened windows.

Her hands, which had started to push him away, gathered up bunches of the cotton shirt. Her lips parted, seemingly of their own volition, acquiescing to his husky request.

"Ah, Jess." His relief was expelled on a deep breath that shuddered out of his mouth and into hers. "I promise, I won't hurt you. Not ever."

But he would, she knew, as she allowed herself to be pulled into the misty world of desire he was offering her. Oh, not physically. His touch, as his hands roamed her back, was as gentle as his lips were tender. This man, whoever he was, was nothing like Eric Chapmann. He would never rape and plunder, but only take what she gave willingly.

The problem, Jessica feared, was that she was perilously close to offering up her heart along with her body. And once she did that, she knew that the danger would be all too real.

Even as she knew all that, Jessica couldn't stop her heart from fluttering or her lips from responding. The scrape of his teeth against her bottom lip warmed her blood and caused her to moan softly, inviting him to deepen the kiss. Which he did. Gloriously.

And as his tongue engaged hers in a sensual mating, and his hands skimmed down her sides, his thumbs brushing against her breasts, she felt every joint in her body become fluid. No longer certain she could stand on her own, Jess clung to him, willing to go wherever he took her.

She was trembling in his arms. Her lips had softened and clung to his, inviting so much more. Her body was molded so tightly against his that Rory was vividly, painfully aware of every slender curve and valley.

Rory was surprised at how vulnerable she'd allowed herself to be. How defenseless. He wanted her. Lord, how he wanted her! But not this way.

When she came to him, and Rory had not a single doubt that she would, he wanted her to come knowing exactly who he was. And, more to the point, who she was. He wanted her to come, he realized reluctantly, not out of desire, but love.

Although it was the hardest thing he'd ever done, he managed, just barely, to surrender the delicious taste of her lips and to put her a little away from him.

"You didn't say no," he reminded her.

"I didn't say yes."

"Didn't you?"

She yanked her hands from his chest and glared up at him, furious that he could remain so calm when she was not. "You think this is some kind of joke, don't you?"

Her tone was icy, at odds with the fire in her eyes. That contrast between frost and flame was what had drawn him to his Emilie in the first place. It was what made him realize, more than ever, that somehow he'd been given a second chance.

He took hold of her wrist and, pressing her hand against the placket of his jeans, gave her graphic proof of his rampant need.

"This isn't any joke. I want you, Jess. There aren't any words for how much, although *desperately* comes close. And, believe me, although I've never been a man to make noble gestures, I'm making one tonight."

She could literally feel his raw, masculine life force pulsing beneath her fingertips. It took every ounce of self-restraint Jessica possessed not to unbutton those jeans and take him in her hands, her mouth. . . .

"You know," he murmured, "if you keep caressing me like that, sweetheart, all my good intentions are going to fly right out the window."

She jerked her hand away. "I'm sorry."

"Not as sorry as I am." His voice and his eyes were filled with a lazy humor Jess found far too appealing.

"I don't understand what's happening to me."

"I felt the same confusion, in the beginning."

"You're still confused," she insisted. "You think it's 1896, you believe you're Rory Mannion—"

"I am Rory Mannion."

Jessica ignored his quiet interjection. "You believe Eric Chapmann is some horrid nineteenth-century gunman who murdered your wife. And you believe I am your wife! Hell, next thing I know Rod Serling is going to pop into the kitchen and welcome me to the Twilight Zone."

"Who is Rod Serling?"

"I give up!" Jessica threw up her hands.

Since willingly surrendering her virginity during her freshman year of college, Jessica had always managed to separate sex from love. Although she'd never thought of herself as promiscuous, she possessed the ability to treat sex as a pleasant recreational activity. She always felt warm affection for the men she went to bed with, including and especially Trace Callahan, and when the affair was over, they'd go their separate ways, most of the time remaining friends.

But on some deep, instinctive level she knew that with this man it would be different. Rory Mannion would never settle for a piece of her life. With him, it would be all or nothing.

Determined to regain control of the situation, she took two soup bowls from the cupboard, began filling them and was appalled that her hands were trembling so badly, the red broth spilled over the stove top and sizzled on the burner.

"Perhaps I could help." He took the ladle from her nerveless fingers and began dishing out the soup with annoying composure.

"How can you remain so damn calm?" she flared. "How can you make it seem so easy?"

Rory knew they were not discussing filling the soup bowls. "It's not at all easy. But I'm not certain it should be," he decided. "I remember how we both knew the moment we met, when I showed up to arrest you—"

"You were going to arrest Emilie? Why?"

He smiled at the memory. "It's a long story. I'll tell you over dinner." Perhaps, Rory thought with satisfaction as he put the bowls on the table while she managed to spoon the lasagna onto plates without spilling it onto the floor, the story would trigger her memory.

And then, once she recalled who she was, Rory was going to take her up to that ultrafeminine bedroom and make mad, passionate love to her. Again and again until she remembered all the reasons they belonged together. For all time.

6

TO JESSICA'S AMAZEMENT and vast relief, she found herself enjoying Rory's story. The trick was, she decided, to treat it like a movie or book plot he was relating, and not an actual incident from some impossible past life.

"Do you know," she said suddenly, "you've reminded me of a notice I saw in the *Rim Rock Record* a few days ago. There's a showing of old photographs and woodcuts at The Road to Ruin."

"The Road to Ruin? Why would there be an art show at a brothel?"

"A brothel? Oh. That's right. You're still stuck in 1896."

"Actually, I'm stuck in 1996," he corrected. "But my knowledge is a century behind the times."

"I've heard that happens a lot in time travel," she said dryly. "Anyway, The Road to Ruin is a gallery owned by Noel Giraudeau."

"Giraudeau?" The name was vaguely familiar.

"Of Montacroix. Her brother is regent. She moved here a few months ago. She's a lovely woman. She and Mackenzie Reardon, publisher of the *Rim Rock Record*, are engaged to be married. Her family wants the ceremony in Montacroix, you know, with all the bells and whistles—"

"Whistles at a wedding?"

"I was speaking figuratively. I suppose I should have said pomp and circumstance."

"Ah." Rory nodded. That he understood.

"Anyway, since she's pregnant, Mac doesn't want her to travel all that way, although I have to admit there is something to be said for getting married in a palace."

"Is that your desire?" he wondered curiously.

They'd gotten married in the meadow behind the new home he'd built her. Although her attire had been deemed controversial, Rory had never seen anything as lovely as his young bride, looking beautifully ethereal in a gown of sheer white pin-dotted swiss and a coronet of wildflowers in her free-flowing blond hair. She'd reminded him of a fairy from one of Hans Christian Andersen's tales.

"Actually, I have every intention of remaining single."

Rory, who could not envision such a vibrant woman living without a man, thought that was about the saddest statement he'd ever heard. "Why?"

"Because I have no intention of becoming a meek, quiet, accommodating woman who turns all her energies to various charities. Not that charity work isn't important," she allowed. "It's just not how I choose to live my life."

"Not all wives become meek."

"I suppose not," she admitted as Mariah Swann Callahan immediately came to mind.

Jessica had thought that she'd escaped her father's influence on her life by coming west. Lately she'd begun to realize that all the men she dated—with the exception of Trace—were the kind of men willing to grant her entire control over their relationships. It was, she'd decided, the way she wanted it.

"I do know that if I ever decide to get married, it will be to a man who lets me wear the pants in the family."

"You look very nice in pants," Rory said, immediately recalling those tight wet jeans. "But you also look very appealing in skirts."

His gaze was warm enough to melt both polar ice caps. As she found herself falling under its sensual spell again, Jessica reminded herself that with or without amnesia, this was not a man who could be easily handled. Which meant, she reminded herself firmly, that he was definitely not her type.

"I think we should get back to Emilie," she said briskly, changing the subject before she found herself in water over her head. "Tell me more about her photographs."

Understanding what she was doing and deciding that her caution was warranted for now, Rory told her about how his wife's mother had died in childbirth, leaving her to the care of her father, a man not given to staying in any one place very long. He'd traveled the world, taking photographs of far-off places, and although he'd tried to keep his daughter safe in the care of various aunts, she would always run away to be with him.

"Finally, when she was ten, he surrendered and allowed her to accompany him on his travels." Rory smiled, as he always did, when he pictured his bride as she must have been—a willowy child with a will of pure steel. "Emilie became his assistant on the trip where he photographed the worker driving the last spike into the track of the Canadian Pacific Railroad.

"From Canada they went to South Africa to photograph the gold rush there, then to Greece for the first Olympic games, then up to the Yukon for that gold rush."

"That's a lot of traveling for a little girl."

"Her relatives fought against his taking her to so many remote locations, but there was no way she'd stay home. And while James Cartwright—that was his name—was supplying photographs for the Pulitzer chain, Emilie began selling her own photographs, giving readers a more personal view.

"Her photo of Orphan Train children being practically auctioned off in Denver appeared on the front pages of the *Saint Louis Post-Dispatch* and New York City's *World* newspapers."

"You sound proud of her."

"Of course I am. She was the most traveled, intelligent woman I'd ever met. And, despite having witnessed so much of man's inhumanity, she managed to remain unrelentingly optimistic. And kindhearted." He smiled at the memory. At Jessica. "She would not hesitate to take a stranger into her house."

Jessica couldn't help smiling back. "I suppose she stopped working after your marriage," she said, once again forgetting that this was just a fanciful story born in his poor damaged mind.

"Why would she do that?" He looked at her with honest surprise.

"I doubt many men of the time allowed their wives to have careers."

He laughed at that, a rich, bold sound filled with humor. "I would have liked to have seen the man who could have taken Emilie's beloved camera away. As for wives working, every woman I ever knew worked side by side with her husband, helping to build a life for themselves and their families."

He rubbed his chin. The stubble was beginning to get on his nerves. "Surely you didn't believe that it was only the men who won the West?"

"Of course not. But from the way women have been systematically left out of the history books, I have to assume that the men of the time, who were writing those books, didn't believe in giving their accomplishments any true credit."

"Not all the men of my time believed women to be inferior in any way. I certainly didn't."

Their eyes met and held. And in that suspended moment, Jessica was forced to ask herself why she felt that strange sense of familiarity.

Rory Mannion simply reminded her of someone she'd met in the past, she assured herself. That was the obvious—and logical—explanation.

"Tell me about your work," Rory said as the silence lingered.

"My work? Why?"

"Because I'm interested. After all, we're both in the same profession, so to speak. I was a lawyer before I was a marshall. Then it was my job to bring criminals to justice, while yours, it appears, is to make certain they remain in jail."

"That's the way it's supposed to work, anyway." Jessica frowned as she thought of Eric Chapmann.

"Don't think of him," Rory said quietly, proving yet again an eerie ability to read her thoughts. "Not tonight. Not when we're having such an enjoyable evening."

He was right. Although she still refused to believe that Rory had somehow traveled through time to this century, she could not deny the bond that seemed to have been between them from the beginning. The bond that was growing stronger.

Conveniently ignoring the fact that he couldn't really be the marshall of Arizona Territory, which in turn meant that they really didn't have their work in common, she proceeded to tell him about her current caseload, which included the usual teenage vandalism like mailbox bashing and firecracker damage; some break and enters; the typical weekend drunk and disorderly; a drunk driving case which was being heatedly challenged by the accused, a Hollywood Hunk of the Month who'd been filming a made-for-television movie in Whiskey River last month; and two domestic violence cases, which were two more than she would have liked.

"As you can see," she said, "it's not exactly a big-city caseload. But we're starting to see crimes more typical to Phoenix or Tucson."

Like the methamphetamine lab Trace had busted last month. Fortunately, neighbors accustomed to the pristine pine-scented mountain air had complained of the fumes, which resulted in the lab's being shut down before a customer base had been established.

"Would you prefer working in a big city?" Rory had no doubt she was intelligent. And she seemed to be ambitious, which, he supposed, could only mean moving away from Whiskey River to more high-profile crimes.

She surprised him by laughing at that. "Not on a bet. We had a high-profile case a few months ago. A senator's wife, Laura Swann, was murdered. The fact that she was pregnant at the time with her lover's child only added to the prurient interest in the case. Although Trace, as sheriff, got the majority of the press flak, I had enough to make me realize that I'd lucked out when I'd thrown that dart at the map and ended up in Whiskey River."

"You chose your new home by throwing a dart at a map?"

"It seemed as good a way as any. But I have to admit I cheated. I tore the map in two at the Mississippi River and threw the eastern half away."

"Why?"

"If you'd ever met my father, you wouldn't ask that question," she said dryly. But there was real affection in her tone. "He's a federal judge in Philadelphia. He's the most intelligent man I've ever met. Also the most domineering. He's always ruled his home, including his family, with the same iron hand he rules his courtroom. And although I do truly love him dearly, I knew if I didn't escape his influence, he'd try to run my career. And my life."

"And now you believe a strong man might try to control you the same way in marriage."

"That seems to be how it works," Jessica muttered, wishing they'd stop straying back to the *M* word.

She was wrong, of course. But Rory's head had begun to ache again and he didn't feel up to arguing the point.

"I'd be interested in visiting this Road to Ruin gallery," he said, reverting to the earlier topic. "Do you think we could go tomorrow?"

She'd planned to spend the weekend catching up on the work she'd missed. But it occurred to her that if he actually saw photographs from the 1890s he might be more willing to accept that his belief he was from that time was merely a trick of an injured mind.

"I think that's a lovely idea," she said.

They exchanged a smile. And then, as she watched a shadow move over his eyes, she realized that the pain had returned.

She reached out and covered his hand with hers. "Let me get you another pill."

"No." He linked their fingers together. "I don't want any more drugs."

"But you're in pain."

"I've been shot before," he surprised her by revealing. "I've also fallen off my horse before. I can stand the pain. I won't risk becoming an addict, wasting my life in opium dens.

"Besides, I need a clear head to think through what I must do."

"About what?"

"Many things." He lifted their joined hands to his lips. "Such as how to convince you that we're man and wife. And that it's only natural—and legal—to satisfy these feelings we're having."

"Dammit, Rory—"

"Don't worry, Jess," he soothed, smiling against her knuckles. "Unlike Clayton, I would never take a woman against her will. You have no need to be afraid of me."

Although his touch, and that dark, sultry, dangerously sexy look was making her blood hum, Jessica knew he was telling the truth.

"I'm not," she said in a soft voice that was little more than a whisper.

His thumb stroked the sensitive flesh at the inside of her wrist. "Yet your pulse is racing like a rabbit's heart."

"I know." She managed a wry smile. "And to tell you the absolute truth, I am afraid. But not of you."

"Then, of what?"

"Of the way you make me feel." She drew in a deep, shuddering breath. "Of the way I want you."

"Ah, Jess. You've no idea how relieved I am to hear you say that." When his tongue touched a thin blue vein, her pulse leaped in instant, automatic response. "You'll see, my love," he murmured. "There's nothing to be afraid of. Indeed, you always found our tumbles more than enjoyable."

"Dammit, Rory, I'm trying to be understanding here, but you have to stop talking about me as if I were your wife."

"But you are. Or, more to the point, were," he insisted. "I recall one time, when you were taking photographs of a family not far from here, on the Prescott ranch—"

"You know the Prescott ranch?"

"Of course. It was owned by Ezra Prescott during my time."

"Trace lives there now."

"Trace?" Rory stared at her. "He is a Prescott?"

"Actually, he's married to one—Mariah Swann. Her grandmother was Ida Prescott, who left the ranch to Laura Swann, who in turn left it to her sister, Mariah, who recently married Trace."

"Your sheriff is a fortunate man to have married a woman who possesses such good land."

"I believe he considers himself fortunate to have married Mariah for her own sake."

Her tone, which was as dry as a legal brief, flew right over Rory's head. "I can understand that," he agreed easily. "It's how I always felt about you, which brings me back to that day at the ranch. Three days after we were married, a circus came to town, and set up on the property.

"We met there unexpectedly. I'd come to make sure the town rowdies didn't get into drunken brawls with the circus workers and you were there to photograph the events.

"You were intrigued by the sideshow, I remember— the two-headed calf, the Siamese twins, the fat woman who was married to the man whose body was covered with tattoos.

"And then, you discovered the sword swallower. He was dressed in a short beaded vest and flowing wide eastern trousers. His chest was bare and deeply tanned from the sun. I watched you watching him, transfixed by the movement of that jeweled piece of steel going deeper and deeper into his mouth, his throat. Your face was flushed, your eyes wide, and when you looked over at me, I knew exactly what you were thinking.

"Without a word, I took you by the hand, and you didn't offer a word of protest, not even when we left your precious camera right there unguarded in the tent. We were nearly overcome with lust and ran to the barn, climbed the ladder into the loft, where the buttery summer sun had warmed the hay and you practically ripped open my trousers, and—"

"I get the picture." Jessica's voice was soft and ragged.

"Afterward, you swore that you'd never forget that day. And I, for one, haven't."

His roughened voice stirred her in ways Jessica didn't want to be stirred. Enticed in ways she was finding impossible to resist.

"It wasn't me," she insisted.

"Of course it was."

He'd planted the seed, Rory thought with satisfaction. Now all he had to do was let it take root in her fertile mind.

"I'm suddenly very tired." He released her hand, pushed back his chair and stood up. "And as much as I'd love to continue this little stroll down memory lane, I believe it's time I went back upstairs to bed."

"That's a good idea." One more story like that and she'd forget all her good intentions about avoiding any sexual entanglements with this man.

Jessica watched him walk out of the kitchen, listened to the sound of his boots on the stairs. And then, when she was certain she was truly alone, she folded her arms on the table and lowered her head to them.

She reminded herself that he was not her type. He was too strong, too masculine. He was the kind of man who took what he wanted, whatever the cost. The kind of man she'd studiously avoided all of her life.

Every logical atom in her body reminded her sternly that she shouldn't want him.

But want him she did. Madly. Truly.

Desperately.

She went to the den and tried to work but couldn't seem to concentrate, and decided what she needed was a good night's sleep. She had finally managed to fall asleep when the phone rang. Instinctively, she reached out for the bedside table, then realized she was not in bed.

Stumbling around in the dark, she failed to make it to the desk by the fourth ring, and the answering machine clicked on. She listened to her voice instructing the caller to leave a message, then heard the beep.

"Hey, Jess, sweetheart, I see you've got your boyfriend staying with you," the all too familiar drawl invaded the midnight darkness. Hearing Eric Chapmann's voice made ice skim up her spine. "I don't know, babe, from what I saw of the guy, he didn't look like he had what it took to satisfy...

"I mean, you always struck me as a very sexy babe. The kind that likes it a little rough. A little hard. Isn't that right, Jessie? You know, while I was sitting in jail, I had lots of time to think about you. About all the things I'd like to do to you.

"I used to look at you, strutting around that courtroom with your lacy bra showing through those silk blouses you like to wear, like some kind of high-priced call girl, and I would kill the time by imagining the sounds you'd make if I took your breasts in my mouth and used my teeth to—"

She snatched up the receiver, intending to tell him that he wasn't frightening her with his juvenile threats when Rory pushed past her and took the receiver from her icy hand.

"You finish that thought and you're a dead man," he growled. "In fact, if you call here again, or try to talk to Jess on the street, or even look at her, I will personally kill you with my bare hands."

He slammed the receiver down onto the cradle, then turned to Jessica.

She was trembling like a willow in a hurricane. The silk nightshirt she was wearing ended high on her thigh and hugged her slender curves like a lover's caress. And although he wanted only to comfort her, Rory had no control over the blood that flooded into his groin at the sight of those long bare legs.

"It's going to be all right," he assured her as he drew her into his arms. She did not resist, but her body was as stiff as a rod of cold steel.

Rory's arms were strong and reassuring, and Jessica forgot that there were dangers involved with being this close.

"Eric Chapmann is the most evil man I've ever met," she murmured into Rory's chest. He wasn't wearing a shirt and his skin felt wonderfully warm and life affirming.

"I know." He gently stroked her hair. "But this time I'm going to stop him. This time he isn't going to hurt you."

"There's nothing you can do."

"That's where you're wrong."

He'd have to kill Clayton, or Chapmann, or whatever he was calling himself these days, Rory knew. Because no matter what he'd said in the pharmacy, Rory had no doubt that some part of Clayton had recognized him. And it wouldn't take long for him to put two and two together and come after Jess. Rory had already allowed the only woman he'd ever loved to die once. He had no intention of letting history repeat itself.

As if reading his mind, she lifted her head. "You won't do anything foolish."

"Of course not." There was nothing foolish about killing a murderer. It was, on the contrary, immensely serious business.

Her eyes were wide and worried in the shimmering silver moonlight streaming through the window. "Promise?"

"I promise." He gave her his most reassuring smile that earned a wobbly one in return, but did not stop her violent tremors. "You're freezing." He ran both his palms up her icy arms. "Let me start a fire in the fireplace and—"

"No!" She pushed against him and backed away. "No fires."

She wrapped her arms around herself in an unconscious gesture of self-protection that tore at his heart. She was obviously more frightened of fire than she'd been of Clayton's threatening call.

And no wonder, Rory thought.

"You're right," he said soothingly as he gathered her back into his arms and pressed a light kiss against her temple. "That's a bad idea."

"I know it's silly." She wrapped her arms around his waist and clung. He could feel her nipples beneath the ivory satin pressing against his chest, and her thighs were tight against his. "But I've always had this irrational fear of fire and . . ."

Her voice drifted off. Rory could literally feel the flicker of comprehension.

She tilted her head and looked up at him, her eyes wide and bewildered. "It can't be."

Her face, in the diffused glow of moonlight, looked pale and fragile. He'd been waiting for her to begin to remember. But this wasn't the time. And it definitely wasn't what he wanted her to recall.

"Shh." He bent his head and brushed his lips lightly across hers. "The middle of the night is not any time for serious discussions."

"But—"

"Later." His mouth lingered over hers, not taking, but giving, bestowing tenderness and reassurance. "Things always look better in the morning."

"I don't understand," she murmured.

"I know." Refusing to let her remain alone in this room that Clayton had defiled with his voice, he lifted her into his arms. When she didn't protest, Rory decided they were definitely making progress. "It takes some getting used to, sweetheart."

She was as light as a feather as he carried her up the stairs. As he entered the bedroom, Rory was reminded of that long-ago evening he'd carried Emilie over the threshold of her new home. He was not the only one who remembered.

"We've done this before," Jess murmured groggily as he laid her gently, almost reverently on the bed. "I remember being nervous." Her eyelids drifted shut. "I knew you were experienced. I'd heard stories about the girls at The Road to Ruin arguing over who would get to pleasure you and I was so afraid I couldn't measure up."

He hadn't known. If only she'd said something, Rory thought, he could have told her how ridiculous her concerns had been.

"You were the only woman I'd ever loved." Knowing he was playing with fire, but unable to resist, he slipped into bed beside her. "And you were perfect."

"That's so sweet." When he would have kept his distance, she tested his resolve to its limits by snuggling up against him and pressing her smiling lips against his throat. "I remember thinking you were lying. . . ." Her breathing was becoming deeper, her words spaced further apart.

He pressed his lips against her hair. "I'd never lie to you."

"I think—" she threw a long slender leg over his "—that you did. But it was a sweet lie . . . so I was prepared to forgive you. . . . Then your hands began to move over me—" she sighed happily with the memory "—and I forgot whatever it was." Her fingers twined around his neck. "What I was forgiving you for."

She was as close as any one person could possibly get to another. Her body was soft and warm; Rory could feel the heat through the silk nightshirt that had risen almost to her waist, revealing a pair of silk underpants so skimpy he wondered why she even bothered with them.

As his body throbbed with a masculine hunger that had been denied too long, Rory decided that it was going to be a very long night.

7

RORY WAS AWAKENED by the sound of music. Confused, he looked around for the source. "What the blazes?"

"It's the clock radio," Jessica murmured sleepily, reaching over to hit the Sleep button, muting the sound.

She glanced up at him. His eyes were clear from pain this morning and even with his four-day-old beard, he was the most handsome man she'd ever seen.

"I think this is where I'm suppose to leap out of bed and pretend to be embarrassed," she said.

"Are you embarrassed?"

"I don't think so." Strangely, her mind seemed to be operating on two levels. One part was appalled that she was lying in bed with a strange man. Another part, the side that was winning, found the experience extremely pleasant.

He smiled at that. "That's a very good beginning."

"I am confused."

"I know that feeling. Very well."

"And now you're not?"

"I don't understand how I came to be in your time, but I know why I'm here."

He sounded so sure of himself. Jessica still found the idea of time travel incredible. However, when you

stopped to think about it, so were faxes, organ trans-
plants and the Internet. And the government was
spending a fortune trying to discover life on other gal-
axies. Why wasn't it possible to transcend the bounds
of time?

"Why?"

"That should be obvious." He cupped her cheek in
his palm. "To be with you, of course." And to avenge
Emilie's murder, but this comfortable, lazy morning did
not seem the time to bring up that unpleasant subject.

"You can't really believe I'm Emilie."

Rory shook his head. He'd given the matter a great
deal of thought during the night as she'd slept in his
arms and realized that Jessica Ingersoll was not the
same woman he'd married.

"I believe," he said slowly, thoughtfully, "that you
and Emilie both possess the same spirit. But your
unique life experiences, and the different time in which
you live, have made you a distinct individual.

"There is much of Emilie in you, Jessica Ingersoll. But
you're still very much your own woman." He stroked
her cheek with the pad of his thumb. "A woman I find
very appealing."

His body was warm against hers. And hard. Jessica
could feel his erection against her belly and realized that
if she just moved a smidgen . . .

No! Sleeping in the same bed with the man on such
short acquaintance was bad enough. Having sex with
him would be a huge mistake. But dear heavens, she

thought as she read the blatant desire in his darkening gaze, how she was tempted!

"The ideas of time travel and reincarnation are a bit much for me to handle before my morning coffee." She tried for a breezy, flippant tone and knew she wasn't fooling either of them for a moment. "I think I'll take a shower and—"

Her words were cut off in midsentence by the ringing of the phone. She stiffened instinctively.

Understanding her fear, Rory reached out and scooped up the receiver. "Who is it?" he growled.

There was a pause on the other end of the line. Then a muffled curse Rory recognized immediately.

"It's Trace Callahan." The sheriff's words sounded as if they were being spit through clenched teeth. "I need to speak with Jessica."

Given the fact that it was a man's duty to protect women, and since Jess seemed to have no male in her life to fill that role, Rory understood, and accepted, Callahan's less than cordial attitude.

"It's the sheriff." He handed the receiver to Jessica.

She grimaced and prepared herself for the barrage. "Hi, Trace," she said with feigned brightness. "What's up?"

"What the hell is that guy doing in your house?"

Jessica was grateful that picture phones had not come to Whiskey River. She figured if Trace could see that Rory was not only in her house, but her bed as well, he'd probably blow sky-high.

"We discussed this yesterday, Trace. He needed someplace to stay."

"What about the Silver Spur? That's what motels are for."

When she glanced toward Rory, he realized the conversation was about him. He brushed his lips against her neck, right behind her ear, and murmured, "I believe I'll take a shower."

Jessica watched as he rose from the bed, seeming unconcerned that he was magnificently naked.

"Jess?" Trace demanded. "Are you still there?"

She sighed as the bathroom door closed. "Yes. And I suppose the prudent thing to do would have been to take him to the motel. But it could have been dangerous for him to be all alone. What if he'd had a relapse?"

"You're not his doctor. Or his nurse."

"I know." Jessica wondered what Trace would say if she told him that Rory believed that she was his wife. "But this seemed right, Trace."

He cursed. A short pungent oath ripe with aggravation. "You're the most stubborn woman I've ever met."

"Actually, I believe that crown goes to your lovely wife," she said easily. "But I'd be proud to be runner-up." She heard the shower turn on, pictured Rory standing beneath the stream of warm water and tamped down a sudden, irrational desire to join him. "Did you call to lecture me about my houseguest? Because if you did—"

"I called about Chapmann."

The bedroom was warm but Jessica felt a sudden chill. "What about him?"

"I heard your so-called houseguest threatened him yesterday in Otterbein's pharmacy."

"Chapmann was making veiled threats. Rory was merely trying to protect me."

"That's the way Walter tells it," Trace allowed. "But he mentioned something about Mannion confusing Chapmann with Clayton."

When she didn't immediately answer, he said, "Jess? Is that true?"

"It's true, but—"

"Dammit, the guy's nuts. And he's in your house!"

His roar reminded her of a wounded lion. Jessica put the receiver a little away from her ear. "You should be glad he is," she said. "Chapmann threatened me again last night. If Rory hadn't been here—"

"He threatened you? How? When?"

"Sometime in the middle of the night. He woke me up and made lewd suggestions on my answering machine. I was going to bring you the tape this morning, on the way to The Road to Ruin."

Trace groaned. "Don't tell me that you're actually taking Mannion to see Emilie Mannion's photographs."

"It's the best way to straighten all this out."

"Or make him even more delusional."

"What if he's not?"

"Not what?"

"What if he's not delusional?"

There was a long pause on the other end of the phone. "You're not suggesting that the guy really did somehow zap through time and end up here in the twentieth century, are you?"

"I'm not suggesting anything," she hedged. "I was merely pointing out that some situations are too complex for easy answers."

There was another long pause. "I worry about you," he said finally.

"I know." Her voice softened. "That's your fatal flaw, Callahan. You worry about everyone."

"You more than most."

She smiled and felt her eyes misting up. "I know that, too. And trust me, Trace, if I didn't believe I was entirely safe with Rory, I wouldn't let him stay here."

"Make sure you stop by the office on the way to the gallery," he said, knowing her well enough to know when arguing any further would be futile. "I want to hear that tape. And Jess—"

"Yes?"

"Be very, very careful, okay?"

"Okay." Despite the pall the subject of Chapmann had put over her morning, Jess was smiling when she hung up the phone.

"Is that true?" a deep voice asked.

She turned and saw Rory standing in the doorway between the bedroom and bathroom. The contrast between his hard masculine body and her lace-trimmed towel was enough to make any feminine heart flutter.

"Is what true?" she asked with what she thought was considerable aplomb, considering the circumstances.

"Is it true that you feel entirely safe with me?"

She considered lying and knew she'd never get away with it. "In the way Trace meant, yes."

"Meaning you trust I won't murder you in your sleep."

Jess nodded.

"But in that other, more fundamental way—"

"I'm still afraid," she admitted. "I've never felt like this about any other man and I'm not certain I like it."

He surprised her by laughing at that.

Hurt by his response, Jessica lifted her chin. "I didn't realize I'd said anything humorous."

His expression immediately sobered. Affection warmed his whiskey-hued eyes to a deep chocolate brown. "You didn't. Not really."

He crossed the carpet, stopped in front of her and framed her frowning face between his hands. "What you said was, word for word, what Emilie told me the first day we met."

"Oh."

Warmth flowed from his fingertips beneath her flesh, spreading outward throughout her body like shimmering gold summer sunshine. She gathered up handfuls of the sheet and curled her hands into fists, to keep from ripping that towel away.

"I suppose it's not all that original a thing for a woman to say to a man she finds herself unwillingly attracted to."

"I suppose not."

She looked so sweet. So flustered. Rory knew it would not take much to entice her into spending the morning amidst those rumpled sheets and by the time he was finished, she'd remember everything.

But he could also tell that there was a part of her that was holding back. And until she could come to him willingly, without a single reservation, he was willing to wait.

"Is there a barber in town these days?"

"Of course." His hair, which curled over his collar, was admittedly a little shaggy, but personally she liked it that way.

"Good." Rory nodded his satisfaction as he rubbed his palm down the side of his face. "I feel as if I've been on a month-long trail ride. I need to get a shave before meeting your princess gallery owner."

"You don't need to go to a barber for that. You can shave here."

"I didn't see a razor or strap in your bathroom."

"That's because you weren't looking for the right thing."

She got out of bed. Rory followed her into the bathroom and decided that the sight of her hips moving beneath that silk nightshirt was about the most erotic thing he'd ever seen. Even more enticing than that painting of the nude nymph hanging on Belle's parlor wall at The Road to Ruin brothel.

"Here it is."

He looked down at the small pink razor she was holding out to him. "You can't expect a man to shave with such a thing."

"Why not? I'll admit it's not exactly a masculine color, but—"

"It's too flimsy." He took it, hefted it in his hand and frowned.

"I shave my legs with it every day," she assured him. "It's got a flexible double blade and an aloe moistening strip. You'll love it."

He continued to look unconvinced. "Perhaps you should shave me this first time. To show me how it works."

"You're an intelligent man. Surely you can figure it out for yourself."

"I have no doubt I could. Eventually." He idly moved the feminine razor from one hand to the other. "However, I would hate to meet your friend, the royal princess, with bandages all over my face."

"Talk about your con jobs," she muttered.

"You're accusing me of running a confidence scheme?" He placed a hand against his chest and gave her his most innocent look. "You're an intelligent woman, Jess. A man would be foolhardy to try to put anything over on you."

She gave him another long look. "Cute, Mannion," she muttered. "Real cute." She gestured to a small velvet stool beside the sink. "Sit down and let's get this over with."

Smiling his satisfaction, Rory did as instructed, and watched as she turned on the water and picked up a green can. "Aerosol," she said as she pressed the top of the can, causing a cloud of white foam to spew forth. She wet his face, then filled her hand with the foam and began spreading it over his cheeks, chin and jaw.

"This is soap?" he asked, imagining smoothing the fluffy cream over her breasts.

He remembered their first week anniversary, when he'd talked Emilie into sharing the large copper bathtub with him. The experience had been more than memorable. But if they'd had soap like this . . .

"It's shaving cream. To soften your beard and your skin."

"Men do not need soft skin."

"Try telling that to any woman suffering from beard burn," she suggested.

"You're very good at this," he said.

"I told you, it's the blade."

"If that's true, perhaps later you will let me return the favor by shaving your legs." He ran his palm up her calf, finding it as smooth as the silk she was wearing.

"Not on a bet."

She trailed the razor down the side of his face, taking a swath of foam, then rinsed it beneath the tap. She managed to shave his cheeks, but ran into trouble when trying to follow the line of his jaw.

"Damn. This is awkward," she muttered, bending over, trying not to nick him while shaving the deep cleft in his chin. "Perhaps you should stand up."

"Perhaps you should sit down." He took hold of her waist and plunked her down on his lap.

"I don't think—"

"The angle is better," he reasoned.

The angle might be better, but the only thing between them was a pair of bikini panties and a towel. Jessica would have felt a lot better if the towel had been made of Kevlar.

"I promise to stay on my best behavior," Rory said, once again seeming to read her mind.

Jessica knew that if Trace could see this, the explosion would undoubtedly be heard all the way to Phoenix. Reminding herself that her personal life was none of his concern, she closed her mind to the thought and continued shaving.

"It is easier," she admitted, leaning over to rinse the razor again.

"Perhaps for you," he muttered as she shifted against the part of him that had been throbbing all night.

She felt him, hot and fully aroused, and a similar heat curled outward from her feminine core. She made one more quick swipe with the razor.

"Done," she announced. And just in the nick of time.

"You did a very professional job," he stated, running his hand over his now smooth cheek.

"Thank you."

He was still holding her on his lap and his firmly cut lips were just a whisper from hers. She knew, from the sexy gleam in his eyes, that Rory wanted to kiss her. And that was just for starters.

"Did you say something about stopping by the sheriff's office on the way to the gallery?" he asked.

Jessica was both grateful and disappointed when he effectively shattered the mood of shared desire that had settled over them. She wanted him. She also had not a single doubt that he wanted her, too. But she realized that he was willing to wait until her head caught up with her heart. And her rebellious, needy body. And for that alone, she loved him.

Love? The word tolled like a warning bell in her head. She was attracted to him, fascinated by him, cared more than she should for him. But could she actually be in love with him?

Of course not, the logical mind that had graduated with honors at the top of her law school class insisted.

Maybe, another, equally pragmatic part of her that was willing to look at all sides of a problem suggested.

Oh, yes, the romantic she'd never known was dwelling inside her whispered.

It was the romantic that stayed with her all during her lonely shower. The romantic that had her choose a short winter-white wool skirt, matching tights and a pink angora sweater instead of her usual Saturday wardrobe of jeans and a sweatshirt.

And it was the romantic who spent a blissful hour at the Branding Iron Café, her stack of blueberry pancakes going almost untouched, as Rory enthralled her with stories about the old West.

Wild, wonderful tales of Rory Mannion's life and times that were much the same as those in the book she'd borrowed from the museum, but far more detailed. Jessica was sorry when it came time to leave—time to return to the real world which included the answering machine tape she had to give to Trace.

She managed to convince Rory to stay in the car while she ran the tapes into the courthouse and up the stairs to Trace's office, where she was submitted to yet another lecture about the dangers of letting a strange man stay in her house. From his frustrated behavior, she suspected Trace would have loved to have locked her safely away in a cell if he could only have figured out a charge he could make stick.

And then they drove the two blocks to The Road to Ruin. As they entered the gallery, and the bell on the door chimed, Jessica realized she was holding her breath.

Noel Giraudeau was in the process of hanging a group of framed photographs on the cream wall. A yellow dog the size of a small pony lay at her feet. She turned at the sound of the bell and greeted the couple with a smile.

"Jessica, what a nice surprise." She held out both her hands. "It's been too long since we've had a chance to visit."

"I've been a bit busy," Jessica said.

"I know." Warm blue eyes expressed sympathy. "As Mac wrote in his brilliant editorial, you were robbed in that verdict." The women embraced, exchanging cheek kisses, then Noel turned to Jessica's companion. "Hello."

Her smile froze in place, and Rory watched as the color faded from her face and she began to sway. He took hold of her arms to steady her.

"Are you all right?" Jessica asked, immediately concerned. "Should I call Dr. McGraw?"

"No." Noel shook her head, sending her silky blond hair out in a silvery arc. "I just need to sit down. Perhaps in my office." She gestured toward a nearby door.

Despite the advanced stage of her pregnancy, and the huge yellow dog's growled warning, Rory picked her up and carried her into the office, where he placed her carefully on a love seat covered in a fabric reminiscent of a Navajo blanket. The office windows overlooked a garden ablaze with bright saffron and copper mums. In the middle of the garden a trio of nymphs frolicked in a stone fountain.

"I really think I should call the doctor," Jessica insisted.

"No, I'm fine. Truly." Noel managed a smile. "I was just so surprised...." Her voice drifted off as she stared up at Rory, her expression that of a woman who was looking at a ghost.

"You're Rory Mannion," she said without displaying an iota of the doubt that had been plaguing Jessica. "And you've come for Black Jack."

It was not a question, but Rory answered it anyway. "Yes."

His tone was so hard and implacable it made goose bumps rise on Jessica's arms. "I don't understand," she complained. "How do you know Rory?"

"I don't, not personally. But Mac will, I'm sure."

"Mac?" Jessica was now thoroughly confused.

"It's taken every ounce of feminine persuasion I possess to keep him from doing something drastic about Black Jack's return," Noel murmured. "I truly believe that were it not for the baby—our baby—he would have taken the law into his own hands when Chapmann was acquitted."

"I don't understand any of this," Jessica complained.

"I know." Noel managed an indulgent smile. The color was coming back into her face and her eyes were clearing. "I think it might be better if Mac explained things himself. He publishes the newspaper right next door," she told Rory. "Let me call him and ask him to come over."

Not wanting Noel to get up, Jessica handed her the portable phone from the desk. The call took only a moment and Noel had barely hung up when the ringing of the bell on the door was followed by the sound of boot heels on the polished pine plank floor.

"Are you certain you're all right?" Mackenzie Reardon asked as he burst into the room, his green eyes radiating both love and fear.

"I'm fine." Noel held out a hand to him, which he crushed between both of his.

"You said it was an emergency."

"I said it was important," she correct calmly.

"You said something had happened."

"Yes. But not to the baby. It's about Black Jack."

A thunderstorm moved across his face. "What has that bastard done now? If he so much as spoke to you—"

"No. Not me." She turned their linked hands and pressed her lips against his whitened knuckles in a fond gesture. "We have company, my love," she murmured.

He turned toward Jessica first. "I'm sorry, Jessica. I've heard about the threats Chapmann made to you. If there's anything I can do—" He stopped suddenly as he recognized the man standing beside her. "My God," he said, exhaling a harsh breath, "it's you."

"In the flesh," Rory agreed. Although the appearance was entirely different, he'd recognize his old friend anywhere. "It's good to see you again, Wolfe."

"Wolfe?" Jessica felt as if she'd suddenly fallen down the rabbit hole and ended up at the Mad Hatter's tea party. "Could someone please explain what's going on?"

"It's a little confusing," Noel murmured.

"More than a little," Mac seconded. "In fact, I didn't realize what was happening myself until last month at the Halloween dance, when Noel dressed up in that dance hall outfit and—"

"She's the woman," Rory said with a look of sudden comprehension. "The one you always refused to talk about. The beautiful blonde who mysteriously left Whiskey River after you were cleared of the massacre. The one you swore you'd love until the day you died."

"For eternity," Mac said. He exchanged a fond, loving look with Noel, then turned to Jessica, his green eyes looking deep into hers, as if he were looking straight into her soul. "This gets more and more amazing," he murmured.

"You can say that again," Rory agreed, knowing that his old drinking and card-playing buddy was beginning to realize that Emilie had come back as well, making the circle complete.

"I think," Noel said, looking at a bewildered Jessica with sympathy, "we should all sit down and have some tea. And since Mac is the storyteller of the group, I believe he should be the one to explain the situation to Jessica."

"Good idea," Rory agreed. He pulled up two chairs, one for himself and one for Jess. Taking hold of her hand, he nodded toward the man he'd known a hundred years ago as Wolfe Longwalker.

8

"THIS IS IMPOSSIBLE!"

Jessica stared at the newspaperman she'd always known as Mackenzie Reardon, the man who'd given up a prestigious job as editor of the *Chicago Sun-Times* to return to his hometown and become publisher and editor of the small circulation *Rim Rock Record*. For thirty minutes this intelligent, soft-spoken individual had told her things that defied belief.

"I thought the same thing, when Noel was trying to explain it to me," Mac agreed. "But eventually it sunk in."

"That you're the reincarnation of a half Irish, half Navajo writer who fell in love with a psychic princess, who'd inherited the gift of second sight from her Gypsy grandmother. A princess who just happened to have a vision of you all the way across the sea in her own kingdom—a hundred years later!

"And despite the fact that she was supposed to be preparing for her wedding to another man, flew to Arizona, drove to Whiskey River, and stayed at The Road To Ruin, which had been turned into a bed-and-breakfast. Then she bought a book written by Wolfe Longwalker—you—and this mysterious book magically zapped her backward in time to save you from hanging, then returned to the present to wait for you?"

"I had no idea Wolfe would return," Noel explained. "I was honestly prepared to spend the rest of my life alone.... Well—" she patted her bulging stomach "—not exactly alone."

"That's right," Jessica said dryly. "You returned to the twentieth century carrying Wolfe Longwalker's baby."

"I've always considered that a miracle," Noel said with the serenity that she wore like a second skin in spite of her rollicking adventure in 1896 Whiskey River.

"It's definitely the world's longest pregnancy." Jessica shook her head in disbelief. "You really should call the Guinness people. You'd definitely end up with the world's record."

"I don't pretend to understand how it happened, but it's true," Noel insisted quietly. "The minute Mac came up to the house to interview me for the *Record*, I recognized him. Even without the birthmark."

"Birthmark?"

"Wolfe Longwalker was born with a mark in the shape of a wolf's head on the inside of his wrist." Noel smiled at her husband-to-be. "Show her, darling."

Mac obligingly rolled up his sleeve and held out his arm, revealing the mark.

"It could be a coincidence," Jessica insisted doggedly.

"That's what I tried to tell myself at first," Mac said, the warmth in his gaze revealing that he definitely empathized with Jessica's confusion. "But I remembered too many things that weren't in any history texts. Intimate things about Noel's visit to Arizona Territory that only a lover would know." He exchanged a loving gaze with his fiancée, who blushed in response.

"It also explained," he said, "why I had the sudden urge to leave a successful big-city career, where presidential candidates vied for my endorsement, to return home and spend every last cent of my savings to buy a paper that's always drowning in red ink and has the huge staff of two reporters and one part-time photographer."

"Are you telling me that you believe that you came home because you somehow knew that the woman you'd loved in a previous century had moved here?"

"On some intuitive level, absolutely. As I said, from the moment I first saw Noel, working in her garden, I knew she seemed familiar. But I managed to convince myself that I recognized her from all the photographs that have appeared in magazines over the years.

"But when I saw her in the duplicate of the dress she was wearing when she saved my life, it all came flooding back to me. Including the part about Black Jack and his pals framing me for murders I didn't commit."

He looked over at Noel again. "I still wish you'd killed him when you shot him in The Road to Ruin."

"The brothel, not this gallery," Noel answered Jessica's unspoken question. "And considering how horribly guilty I felt when I'd thought I had killed him, I can't agree with that, Mac."

Mac muttered a curse and folded his arms across his chest. "Then I should have killed him."

Jessica was staring at the pregnant woman the tabloid press had dubbed The Ice Princess, to differentiate between her and her more flamboyant sister. "You actually shot a man?"

"To save Wolfe's life," Noel confirmed.

"Amazing." That was the most incomprehensible thing she'd heard thus far. "So, continuing down this very strange path, Mac is Wolfe, Noel is the same person she always was, Rory is still Rory, Eric Chapmann is Black Jack Clayton, a notorious cold-blooded killer, and I'm supposed to be Emilie Cartwright Mannion."

"That's it in a nutshell," Mac agreed.

"It all appears to fit," Noel said.

"I told you." This from Rory.

Jessica dragged her hand through her hair. "But I don't remember anything."

"Of course you do," Rory said gently. "Just little flashes, but I've seen them."

"That's the way it worked for me," Mac offered. "In the beginning. May I ask you something?"

"Shoot." Jessica's sense of humor returned and she grinned at Noel. "I was speaking figuratively."

Noel returned Jess's smile with a friendly, reassuring one of her own. "I know."

"How did you end up in Whiskey River?" Mac asked.

"Simple. I wanted to get as far away from Philadelphia as I could."

"That would be California. Or Alaska."

"I'm afraid of earthquakes. And weeks of darkness would get depressing."

"Why Whiskey River?" he asked again. "An attorney with all you have going for you could probably end up state attorney general if you practiced in a big city."

"Maybe I like small towns." She knew her tone was overly defensive, but couldn't help herself.

"There are a lot of small towns between here and Philadelphia."

"All right. I threw a dart. I'll admit it's not a very intelligent way to choose a career location, but that's what I did."

"Isn't it strange," Noel murmured, "how fate works?"

"You can't be suggesting that some sort of fate or destiny had us all showing up here together?"

"I've come to think of Whiskey River as being a bit like Brigadoon," Noel said. "Hidden away here in the mists, just waiting for those who understand its magic to discover it."

Magic, time travel, mists. It was all too much for someone who'd always prided herself on possessing an analytical, logical mind.

"I don't want to insult you all," Jessica said. "But I still feel as if we've eaten some sort of funny mushroom and landed in the same hallucination."

"You remembered last night," Rory reminded her quietly. "You talked about our wedding night, about how you'd worried about measuring up to the working girls at The Road to Ruin. And although I'd reassured you that you were perfect, you thought I must be lying."

"I didn't—"

"It was right before you fell asleep. After Clayton called you were trembling and ice-cold, so I offered to light a fire to warm you up, but you told me how frightened you were of fires, so I didn't. You almost remembered, but I was grateful you hadn't, because it must have been horrendous.

"So I carried you upstairs to bed and you wrapped your arms around me and just before you fell asleep, you remembered—"

"Us being together like that before," she whispered, the memory shimmering in her mind like a mirage just out of reach on the highway.

But what, exactly, was she remembering? Her almost dream? Or the reality of Emilie Mannion's life and death?

"I'm not certain it's wise to push you into remembering," Noel said quietly. "However, if Clayton is making threats against you, it is important you understand the kind of man you're up against."

"I know what kind of man Chapmann is."

"No," the other three said in unison.

"No," Noel repeated, "I don't think you do. Chapmann is dangerous, granted. But he's also clever and rather charming, which is how he manages to convince naive and lonely young women to go off alone with him and juries to acquit him.

"But Black Jack Clayton was purely evil, through and through. I've seen that evil in Chapmann's eyes. And if he begins to remember, and realizes who you are—" her expression was immeasurably grave "—you could be in terrible danger."

"He could use you to get to me," Rory said. "As he has before."

It was truly too much to take in. "So, what do you suggest I do?" Jessica complained. "Go tell Trace that a hired gun from the nineteenth century is going to try to kill me to get back at my husband, who just happens to have tracked the bad guy into this century? He'd probably call for a straitjacket."

"You've already told the sheriff that Clayton has threatened you," Rory said. "That's all he needs to know at this point."

"It's still so amazing."

"I know." Mac gave her another of those warm reassuring smiles. "It's easier for Noel and Rory, because they've stayed exactly the same people while they've been going back and forth between the centuries. You and I have to reconcile who we are now with who we once were. But believe me, Jessica, we're incredibly fortunate people."

His gaze shifted to Noel and watching the depth of emotion that flowed between them, she felt the sharp pain of a love lost. Which was foolish, because she'd never truly loved anyone in that all-encompassing way.

Or had she? she wondered as she felt Rory's steady presence beside her.

"I think," she said slowly, "I'd like to take a look at Emilie's photographs."

The others remained silent as she walked around the gallery, studying each framed photograph in turn. The subject matter ranged from black-eyed Navajo children to white-haired tribal elders to leather-skinned, bowlegged cowboys, but each shot was intensely personal.

And while Jessica found them both technically wonderful—especially considering the film and equipment restraints Emilie Cartwright Mannion would have been working under—and emotionally eye-catching, not a single shot was even slightly familiar.

Until she got to the one of Rory Mannion, looking wonderfully handsome in a vested black serge suit and stiff white collar. He hadn't gone entirely city, she thought, noting the familiar Stetson and wedge-heeled riding boots. His face, beneath the handlebar mustache, was not smiling.

"My father wanted you to take off that hat," she murmured.

"It's my lucky hat." Rory grinned down at her much as he had on their wedding day.

"That's what you said."

She remembered so much more about that day. How the sun had gilded the grass a pure and gleaming gold in the meadow where they'd exchanged vows; how the scent of wildflowers had filled the air; how Rory's eyes had widened when he'd first seen her in the white dotted swiss dress she'd had a local dressmaker copy from a fashion plate in *Godey's Lady's Book;* how a few of the townswomen had been scandalized at how sheer it was, and at the fact that she'd chosen to wear flowers on her head instead of a proper veil.

She remembered how she'd felt as if she were floating on air as they'd danced the evening away, and later, how he'd introduced her to pleasures beyond her wildest dreams.

Wanting—no, needing—to be alone with him, Jessica turned to Mac and Noel. "I hope you won't think me terribly rude, but I really need to go home."

"Of course." Noel took hold of Jessica's shoulders and kissed her on both cheeks, continental style, as she would her own sister. "If you feel the need to talk about any of this, please call me. Any time."

Jessica knew she meant it. For a woman who'd grown up in a palace, who'd undoubtedly worn diamonds before she'd owned her first pair of jeans, Noel Giraudeau was remarkably down-to-earth. And kind.

"Thank you. I think I may take you up on that."

Still feeling shell-shocked, Jessica left the gallery with Rory. She was already buckled into the leather car seat when she realized Rory had claimed the driver's seat.

"What do you think you're doing?"

"Driving you home."

"You don't know how to drive."

He shrugged. "I've been watching you. It doesn't look all that difficult."

Considering the Jag was an automatic, and the local traffic could never, except during rodeo week, be considered the slightest bit heavy, Jessica decided that it was probably safe enough. However...

"You don't have a license."

"It is necessary to get a license to drive a car?" He turned the key in the ignition. The Jag leaped obediently to life.

"Of course."

"And they call what the Dalton gang does highway robbery," he murmured.

"If you're stopped, you'll get a ticket," she warned.

"Don't worry." He moved the lever, shifting the car into gear. "In the event your sheriff does try to arrest me, I'll merely plead guilty with an excuse."

"And that is?"

He shot her a sideways glance and a grin that possessed the power to melt her heart. "They didn't have drivers' licenses in 1896."

"That's probably because there weren't any cars in Whiskey River in 1896," she said as he pulled away from the curb.

"My point exactly." He flashed her another cocky grin that brightened his eyes and made him look, for the first time since she'd found him lying unconscious on the road, like the warm, funny, loving man who'd tumbled her in a hayloft to the joyful accompaniment of calliope music.

The memory warmed her, but at the same time the images triggered by that photograph of Rory on his—their?—wedding day were terribly unnerving. Dangerous or not, Jessica was grateful that Rory had insisted on driving.

Rory quickly understood why the automobile had replaced the horse. Although there was much to be said for horses, and he'd been extremely fond of his mare, the ability to cover ground at such speed was not only practical but thrilling.

He also understood immediately why Jessica enjoyed driving so fast. The throaty roar of the engine, the sight of the white lines flashing beneath the wheels, the blur of the trees outside the windows were definitely exhilarating.

"I like this driving."

She smiled. "So do I."

He took his eyes from the road long enough to give her an answering smile. "You used to like to gallop."

"I did?" Although she'd lived in Whiskey River for nearly two years, Jessica had never been on a horse.

"You rode like the wind. We used to race along the rim and you beat me more times than I care to admit. And then, after I would lay my ego at your feet and admit defeat, we'd spread out a blanket and have a picnic. You used to fry a chicken and bake the best chocolate cake I'd ever eaten."

"I still make that cake," she said, surprising herself with the memory. "Everyone always says I should enter it at the county fair."

"You won the blue ribbon the year we met. Of course, one of the judges was admittedly prejudiced, but it was still the best cake entered in the contest."

He'd been that judge. Along with Mae Dillon, whose husband owned the mercantile, and Joe Slovik, owner and operator of the livery stable.

"The first time you kissed me was on a picnic," she recalled.

"Actually, the first time I kissed you was at the fair, but that probably doesn't count since you were working the kissing booth at the time."

She blushed at that. "We were raising money to build a library."

"I used up nearly a month's pay."

"I remember." She smiled at the memory of Rory showing up with that long string of tickets. "And afterward, we walked along the midway and you insisted on carrying my camera.

"And you invited me out on that first picnic and I got up hours before dawn to have everything ready. My father thought I was crazy."

"He wasn't at all happy about the idea of another man taking away his apprentice," Rory recalled. "Especially one with my less than sterling reputation. But by the time we got married, I'd won him over."

"That's because you cheated at cards."

"Your father, my love, was a terrible poker player. Cheating was the only way I could make sure he won."

"He knew, you know."

Rory shot her a surprised look. "Really?" And here he'd thought he'd done a pretty damn good job of palming those cards.

"Of course. The first time he took you for twenty dollars, he came home and told me that I should marry you. Because any man willing to lose at poker in the name of love was worth keeping."

Rory laughed. "I liked your father. A lot."

"I know. He liked you, too." She sighed. "I can't believe we're discussing this. My father's very much alive. He's a judge in Philadelphia. He and my mother play bridge on Thursday evenings."

"Is he any good?"

It was Jess's turn to laugh. "He's terrible. Mother's always threatening to get a decent partner."

"There you go," Rory said with a shrug. "It appears that history just keeps repeating itself."

They fell silent for a while, each lost in their own thoughts.

"I wanted you to kiss me that first day when you showed up to arrest me for taking dirty pictures."

"You should have said something. I would have been more than happy to oblige."

"Yet you wouldn't make love to me when I asked you to."

It had been at that same picnic, when she'd been lying beneath him, thrilled by the hard male form pressing against her, dizzy from a sun-filled afternoon of heady, breath-stealing kisses.

"I respected you too much to take advantage of your innocence."

"Even if I wanted you to?"

"It's the man's responsibility to keep a clear head," Rory explained.

And although she found his statement chauvinistic, Jessica decided that if more men felt that way today, there wouldn't be so many single mothers struggling to survive.

"I wanted you more than I'd ever wanted anyone or anything in my life," Rory admitted. "And I needed you more than I'd never needed any woman. But there were two reasons I forced myself from giving in to temptation.

"The first was that I loved you enough to wait until you'd agreed to marry me." Rory recalled all too well how Emilie had forsworn marriage in favor of a career in photography. Fortunately, it hadn't been that difficult to change her mind.

"What was the second reason?"

"I was scared to death of your father."

When she laughed at that, he said, "Hey, the guy was nearly as big as a grizzly bear. He could've crushed me with one swipe of his paw—I mean, hand. It was bad enough that he threatened to kill me if I ever made you cry."

"He didn't!"

"It was on our wedding day. While we were waiting for you to get dressed. He took me aside, welcomed me into the family, then threatened to kick out my lungs and break me into little bitty pieces if I ever did anything to hurt his princess."

"You never said anything about that."

"Why should I when I agreed with him? Hell, I knew that I'd do the same thing if any bastard ever hurt my little girl."

An image flashed through Jessica's mind. Of her father walking her across the meadow to where Rory stood with Wolfe Longwalker, his best man.

She remembered James Cartwright's uncharacteristically gruff voice answering "I do" when the preacher asked who gave this woman in holy matrimony. And she remembered, when he'd kissed her on the cheek, how his eyes had glistened with unshed tears.

Three weeks later, he was dead. Shot in the back by Black Jack Clayton. The next morning Rory had left, to bring Black Jack in. And then . . .

"I can't remember anything after that morning," she murmured. "The morning you rode away."

Rory closed his eyes briefly to ward off the pain, then opened them again to keep from running the car off the road.

"It's probably just as well," he said quietly.

Considering the horrific way you died. The unspoken words hovered in the air between them. And for the first time in her life, Jessica understood her inexplicable fear of fire.

"I've always felt uneasy around Chapmann," she murmured as Rory pulled the Jag into the driveway. "I thought it was merely feminine intuition." But now she realized that it was more than that. Much, much more.

He reached out and pushed the button to open the garage door. As it slowly rose, he turned toward her.

"You realize that this time I'm going to have to do something about him."

"That's Trace's job."

"No." He pulled the car into the garage, stopping it inches from the far wall. "I don't believe in leaving a job unfinished. Even if it takes a hundred years to complete."

Accustomed to his friendly smiles and warm glances, the hardness of his eyes and finality of his tone frightened Jessica.

She put her hand on his arm. "Although every logical instinct I've got tells me that this can't be happening, I have to admit that my heart tells me you're right.

"Somehow, against every law of nature I've been taught to believe in, we seem to have managed to find each other again. So why can't you just be grateful that we've been given a second chance and leave things as they are?"

"Clayton has to pay for his crimes. Surely you felt the same way, or you wouldn't have brought him to trial in the first place."

"That's true. Unfortunately, I didn't do a good enough job, so a jury of his peers acquitted him and he can't be tried again because we have double jeopardy in this country. As we should," she allowed reluctantly.

"The problem is, you're accustomed to old-time western justice, Rory. Give the man a fair trial, then hang him. Isn't that what you said?"

When he muttered something that was part curse, part agreement, Jessica, frustrated, exhaled a ragged breath. "Things aren't so black-and-white these days," she said. "And you'd certainly never get away with killing a man for crimes you say he did a hundred years ago."

"It's not just my word," he reminded her. "Noel and Wolfe—Mac—" he corrected himself "—could corroborate my story. As could you."

"Even if Noel and Mac were willing to say something, which I doubt they would, I'd lose my job if I even suggested such a thing."

She had a point, Rory thought reluctantly. But there had to be some other way to prove his claim in court. "Clayton's murder of Emilie is documented in that book from the museum," he said stubbornly.

"Someday, perhaps, people will accept the idea of time travel, and a lawman will be able to chase a killer through the centuries, like they do in all those Jack the Ripper slasher movies. But right now, it's something reserved for science fiction novels.

"And even if a jury would buy an insanity plea, which I seriously doubt, you could end up spending your life in an institution for the criminally insane." And that, she thought with an inward tremor, she could never allow.

"He has to pay," Rory repeated doggedly.

Jessica wanted to shake him, to scream at him, anything to make him see reason. "Not at the risk of destroying our future."

"I'm going to try my best not to do that."

"And if you fail? What then?"

He leaned over and brushed his lips against hers. "Then I'll just have to keep following him through the centuries until I succeed." He brushed his thumb against her quivering lips. "But I promise, sweetheart, this time Clayton isn't going to get away."

That idea did not give Jessica a great deal of comfort. Because try as she might, she could not envision any way Rory could succeed in his quest without putting his own life in danger.

They'd just entered the house through the garage door leading into the kitchen when the doorbell rang.

After looking out the window and seeing the Floral Fantasy van, Jessica answered the door to the delivery driver, signed on the dotted line on the clipboard he thrust at her, then took the long white box back into the kitchen.

"They're lovely," she said as she turned back the tissue and viewed the long-stemmed red American Beauty roses. "How did you figure out how to order them?"

"I didn't." But from the look of delight on her face, Rory wished he had.

"Then who . . ." She plucked the card from the greenery. "From your secret admirer," she read aloud. "To a woman whose skin is as soft as these petals."

The idea of some other man knowing her that intimately was not a pleasant one.

"This is truly so strange," she murmured.

"You don't know who sent them?" That idea was even less pleasing. Surely she couldn't be involved with that many men?

"I haven't a clue."

The thought occurred to them both at the same time.

Rory opened her briefcase which was lying on the counter and pulled out the pistol she'd told him she kept there. "Keep this close. And call the sheriff," he said, as he plucked the keys from the wooden rack by the door. "Tell him to get over here to guard you right away."

"Rory, you can't—"

He was gone before she could finish the sentence. Jessica heard the car engine, and raced out the front door, in time to see him backing out of the garage, the roof of the Jaguar barely clearing the opening door.

"Oh hell," she muttered.

Afraid of getting Rory in trouble, but even more afraid of the trouble he was capable of getting into by himself, Jessica went back into the kitchen, picked up the phone and called Trace.

9

ERIC CHAPMANN, as Jack Clayton was calling himself these days, was not that difficult to find. Rory guessed that he wouldn't be able to resist sharing the news of this latest intimidation tactic with his cronies.

In the first two bars his search proved fruitless. It was at the third, Denim and Diamonds, a combination western tavern and restaurant, that he found him, playing pool with a pair of men whose hard bodies indicated a lifetime of working the range and whose hard eyes suggested that they'd prove formidable enemies.

The trio was laughing, obviously enjoying Clayton's story. Biding his time until he worked out a plan, Rory was about to order a draft, then realized that he undoubtedly couldn't use his gold pieces to pay for it.

He glanced around the bar. At this time of day it was nearly empty. The only other people in the room were an old man wearing a sweat-stained Stetson whose face had the hue and texture of a raisin, and the woman working as both bartender and waitress. She was wearing a short denim skirt, red handkerchief print blouse, and a fringed denim vest. Her red leather boots, Rory suspected, had never been within a hundred yards of a horse.

Her hair, the color of corn, was piled on the top of her head in a complicated series of twists and curls and lacquered to a rock hard stiffness. She was wearing paint on her eyelids, cheeks and lips, and although the effect was not as garish as the one the girls at The Road to Ruin had favored, Rory much preferred Jessica's understated style.

"What can I get you, honey?" she asked as she returned from delivering an order of long-neck beers to the pool players.

Chapmann, running true to form, had patted her fanny as she'd turned to walk away. Although red flags had waved in her cheeks at the male laughter the cowboy's behavior had elicited, she hadn't uttered a word of complaint.

"Nothing at the moment," he said. "But I would like to speak with you about a private business matter."

She gave him a long look that slowly moved from the top of his hat to the tip of his boots. As her gaze crawled back up again, lingering momentarily on his crotch, Rory suddenly regretted every time in his admittedly less than blameless youth when he'd treated a woman to a similar examination.

"Don't tell me you're the guy from the IRS who keeps sending me all those letters?" she said finally.

"The IRS?"

"I want you to look around." She waved her hand around the nearly deserted bar. "Does it look like I make all that many tips in this place? Granted, the girls working upstairs in the restaurant do okay, but down here it's another story. Now, if I could work nights, maybe you'd have a case, but with no one to watch my kids—"

"I'm afraid I don't understand what you're talking about," Rory interjected into the angry monologue.

"You're not here about last year's income tax return?"

"No." He didn't even know what an income tax return was, and wasn't going to risk another barrage of angry words by asking. "I wanted to speak to you about your customers."

"I should have known it." She nodded and pursed her lips. "You're another one of those private investigators. What are you going to try to do? Get Chapmann on a civil suit?"

"I have no intention of suing anyone."

"Too bad." Her eyes turned hard. "He's one mean son of a bitch when he's been drinking." There was something in her voice and flinty gaze that suggested she had her own reason for disliking the young cowboy. A reason that went beyond a mere slap on the rear.

"He's been upsetting a friend of mine," Rory explained.

"He's good at that," she said. "I take it we're talking about your girlfriend?"

"Yes." Rory decided it would be stretching the truth to call Jess his wife.

"And you intend to stop him."

"Yes."

She gave him another long measuring look. "You're sure big enough. And you look tough enough, if we're talking one-on-one. But in case you haven't noticed, hon, you're a little outnumbered."

"I was hoping you could help me with that."

She chewed on a scarlet nail as she thought that over for a minute. Then she gave him the first smile he'd seen since entering the bar.

"Honey, you're on."

Although he tried to explain he didn't have any money on him to pay for a drink, the woman, who told him her name was Delia, insisted on drawing him a draft.

"You'll call attention to yourself if you're not drinking," she said.

Deciding she had a point, Rory nursed the beer slowly, finding it rather weak and missing the kick he was accustomed to.

The pool players downed the beers Delia had delivered, then called out an order for more, with shots of tequila on the side. Delia cheerfully obliged them, but when Chapmann dipped a finger in the tequila, then ran it along the skin bared by the deep vee of her blouse, she looked to be on the verge of decking him.

Instead, she earned Rory's admiration by laughing and slapping his hand lightly. Then she tousled his dark hair and walked back to the bar on a swivel-hipped stride that even Rory found more than a little appealing.

Ten minutes later the beer began to take effect, and when one of the men headed through the door at the far end of the bar marked Bulls, Delia went to work. While delivering more tequilas—on the house, she assured the men—she began flirting with Chapmann's companion, running her fingers down the front of his shirt, slipping them through the buttons.

Chapmann, who was in the process of clearing the table, looked up long enough to suggest something that Rory couldn't hear, but from the flush that darkened the waitress's cheeks and the way the other man laughed uproariously, he suspected it was definitely sexual in nature.

The cowboy proved to be an easy mark and allowed Delia to lead him out of the room. Rory didn't even want to think about what she'd promised and hoped like hell he could finish Chapmann off before she found herself in more trouble than she could handle.

He moved quickly up behind Chapmann who was lining up a shot designed to put the five ball in the corner pocket.

"You're real good at terrorizing women, aren't you?" he asked quietly.

Chapmann glanced back over his shoulder. "Well, if it isn't the head case boyfriend. What's the matter? You ticked off because that hot to trot lawyer lady called out my name while you were pumping away between those sexy long legs?"

Rory didn't even stop to think. One minute his hand was on Chapmann's shoulder. The next minute, his fist was headed toward the bastard's smug face and he heard the satisfying sound of bone breaking, felt the jaw crush beneath his knuckles.

Chapmann let out a roar like a wounded mountain lion, then swung the pool cue. Rory ducked and Chapmann staggered back, off balance, just as his companion reentered the room. In a split second the cowboy assessed the situation, and bellowing his curses, charged toward Rory.

RORY DECIDED THAT he'd stood a better chance in that bar brawl than he did with a furious Jessica.

"What were you thinking of?" she asked as she paced the floor of Trace's office, her skirt swishing around her thighs. "What if Chapmann had pressed charges?"

"That would have been a bit difficult, since it's not easy talking with a broken jaw," Rory responded. It had been a particularly satisfying moment, almost making up for the pain when Clayton's pal had hit him on the back of the head with a half-empty beer bottle.

"It's not funny, dammit!" She turned on him, her hands on her hips, her voice rising at least an octave higher than its usual throaty tone. "You could have ended up getting arrested. Or even hurt. In case it's skipped your mind, just a few days ago you were lying unconscious in the hospital. You could have been killed."

"Jess." Trace's voice was quiet, but forceful. Rory had realized that the man was an expert at controlling volatile situations when he'd shown up at Denim and Diamonds and immediately put a stop to a fight that had definitely gotten out of hand.

From what Rory had been able to figure out, Jessica had phoned Trace and he'd been at her house when he'd received the call of a fight in progress from Denim and Diamonds. After arriving with Trace at the bar, she'd followed the two men back to the sheriff's in the Jag.

"It's over," Trace told her. "Mannion isn't hurt and Chapmann didn't press charges."

"Only because you threatened him with the answering machine tape," she guessed.

"Whatever works. Within legal limits," he added, then shot a censorious look toward Rory. "You, on the other hand, were definitely out of line."

Rory folded his arms over his chest and met the sheriff's look with a defiant one of his own. "He threatened Jessica. Any man would have done the same thing."

"That's not true," Jessica started to argue.

"Actually," Trace acknowledged, "if I weren't wearing a badge, I would probably have reacted the same way."

Her frustrated gaze went from Rory to Trace, then back again. "You two are unbelievable."

"We both care about you," Rory said. "And we're not going to allow Chapmann to hurt you."

Since she'd already decided that logic didn't work on Rory, Jessica decided to try her other would-be protector. "Talk to him," she begged. "Tell him that taking on Chapmann is dangerous."

"I think he knows that, Jess," Trace said. "And I don't think anything I can say would make any difference."

She shook her head. This was impossible. "Would you at least tell him that he can't kill the man?"

Trace's expression became hard. "She's right about that one, Mannion. Murder's a lot different than breaking a few bones on a guy who needed to be taught a lesson. Don't do the crime if you can't do the time."

Although there was nothing humorous about either the sheriff's words or his expression, Rory couldn't help laughing at that. A short, bitter bark of a laugh.

"Believe me, Sheriff," he said. "Time is the one thing I seem to have plenty of." He turned to Jessica. "I told you not to worry."

She felt the mutinous sting of moisture behind her eyelids and vowed that she would not humiliate herself by crying.

"When we get home, we're going to have a very long talk."

Rory liked the way she made it sound as if her cozy house was his home as well as hers. From the muscle that suddenly clenched in Trace's jaw, Rory suspected the other man was still less than thrilled by their relationship.

Rory understood the sheriff's concern. But he wasn't going to allow it to keep him from spending the rest of his life—however long that turned out to be—with Jess.

"The least you could do," she muttered as they took the elevator down to the first floor of the courthouse, "is check with me before you go breaking up furniture."

"I'm sincerely sorry about that," Rory admitted. Nick McGill, owner of the Denim and Diamonds saloon, had seemed remarkably good-natured, considering the circumstance. "But how does that affect you?"

"I suppose you have a rich fairy godmother who's going to pay to fix those chairs? Not to mention putting new felt on the pool table? And someone's going to have to replace all those bottles that broke when you threw Chapmann over the bar."

Although she'd never admit it, Jessica would have loved to have witnessed that. It would have been just like a movie—*Maverick*, perhaps. Or those wonderful old Clint Eastwood spaghetti westerns she loved to watch on cable television.

"And I suppose you're expecting to be that someone?" He was going to have to find a gold dealer, Rory decided, to find out what his coins were worth these days.

The elevator door opened with a *ding*. "Unless you're planning to ask Mac or Noel, I'm the only person— other than Trace—you know in town."

"I know Chapmann."

"Don't remind me. That's what got us into this mess in the first place. And I doubt if he'd be willing to spring for the repairs. Since according to the witnesses, you swung the first punch."

"Not everyone agrees on that."

"That's right." She stomped down the outside steps toward the Jag, which she'd driven from Denim and Diamonds while Trace had taken Rory to the sheriff's office in the Suburban. "The bartender seems not to have noticed how the brawl started." Her tone was rife with disbelief.

"She was very busy." Rory decided it would not be wise to mention that the bar was nearly deserted.

"She's a woman."

"So?"

"So, she's obviously lying, hoping that it will win points with you."

Rory decided that he liked the fact that Jess seemed jealous.

"Delia's a very nice woman. And she did me a favor when I needed one. But she's not you." He grasped her hand, as she reached to unlock the car door. Then he took her other one, as well. "You should realize by now how I feel about you."

"We've only known each other a few days." Jessica hated the way she sounded so petulant. So needy.

"No." Heedless of the fact that he had a split lip that was swollen and painful, Rory leaned forward and kissed her. A soft, lingering kiss that warmed her blood and clouded her mind. "We've known each other a lifetime," he said against her mouth. "At least two lifetimes, at last count."

She could no longer deny it. During that frantic time when she'd been pacing the floor, waiting for Trace to arrive, memories had flooded back in vivid detail. She remembered the first time they'd met, the amazingly erotic day in that sun-dazzled hayloft, the horror of finding her father dead, shot in the back by Black Jack Clayton because he'd accidentally included the outlaw in a photo, caught in the act of setting fire to a settler's barn.

She remembered, all too well, making love until dawn the night before Rory had gone after Clayton, and how she'd cried as she'd watched him ride away. She remembered pacing the floor of the cabin, desperately waiting for her husband to return.

Which he had. One hundred years later.

She backed away, her heart in her throat. "We'd better go home."

"Yes." He trailed the back of his fingers down her face, pleased as he watched the soft color bloom on her exquisite cheeks. And then, Rory vowed, they would begin making up for lost time.

The mail had come while she'd been at the sheriff's office. Jessica leafed through it, putting the bills in one pile, the catalogs she would look at later in another, and discarding the junk mail. Then she opened a personal card.

"It's from Mariah," she said, reading the brief lines that had been scribbled onto the cream stationery. "Reminding me about the Thanksgiving dinner she suspects Trace forgot to mention. That's a national holiday in a couple weeks," she explained. "You're invited, too." She wondered if Rory's inclusion was the reason that Trace had, indeed, failed to mention the upcoming dinner.

She sounded less than thrilled by the prospect. "If you're afraid I'll embarrass you by getting into a fight—"

"That's not it." She frowned and ran her fingers along the edge of the invitation.

"If I were not here, would you go?"

"Probably," she admitted. "Noel and Mac are invited, too. Along with some other friends—Tara Delaney and Gavin Thomas. It would be good company."

"Yet, I hear a 'but' in your tone."

She dragged her hand through her hair in a nervous gesture he was beginning to recognize. "If we go together, people will think we're a couple."

"I wouldn't have expected you to worry about what people think. Especially friends."

"I never have. But this is different."

"More complicated."

"You can say that again."

She sighed, trying to work up the nerve to ask the question that had been teasing at her mind since Mac and Noel had managed to convince her that Rory was telling the truth.

"What if you're not here for Thanksgiving? What if you end up going back to your own time? As Noel did, when she returned to the twentieth century?"

Leaving the man she loved behind. Jess didn't say the words, but Rory knew she was thinking them. He also understood that she was afraid of giving her heart to him, afraid she'd end up having it broken. As he observed her trembling lips and the moisture sparkling in her eyes, he wished, with all his might, that he could promise that wouldn't happen. But he couldn't.

"Why don't we take things one day at a time?" he suggested gently.

She allowed him to draw her into his arms, and rested her head on his shoulder. "I've suddenly realized I'm a very selfish woman," she murmured into his shirt.

"You couldn't be selfish if you tried." On the contrary, she was the most generous person he'd ever met. In that respect, Rory thought, she was exactly like his Emilie.

"Yes, I am." She looked up at him and touched a hand to his cheek. "Just a few days ago, I had no idea you existed. Now, I can't bear the thought of a life without you."

"Who would have believed we could find each other after so many years?" Rory brushed a snowflake-soft kiss against her tightly set lips. "Whatever happens, we belong together. For all time. We'll find each other again."

Her lips parted beneath his. "If only I could believe that."

"You have to trust me."

She tilted her head back. "I do."

"Good." He gave her a long kiss that stole her breath, then put her a little away from him. "I smell like a brewery from that broken beer bottle. I think I'd better take a shower."

She thought about asking if he wanted company, but worried he'd think her too forward. Although she wanted him and knew he knew it, he was, after all, from a different time. A time when women—nice women— were expected to behave with some decorum.

"You know," he suggested with a cocked brow and a delicious leer, "I could always use some help washing my back. I was, after all, recently wounded."

"Poor dear." Her own eyes gleamed with humor and anticipation. "We'll have to treat you very carefully. With kid gloves, so to speak."

"I think I'd prefer your bare hands." He lifted one of the hands in question and kissed her palm, creating a tingle that went all the way to her toes.

Then, hand in hand, they went upstairs to the bedroom.

"I was so afraid this would be awkward," she murmured as she unbuttoned his shirt. "Because we were strangers."

"But it's not." His own hands made fast work of pulling her sweater over her head. "Because we're not."

"No." She pressed her smiling lips against his bared chest. "We didn't have a shower last time."

"True." At the touch of her lips desire shot to his groin like lightning. She always could make him hot. "But we managed to do all right in the tub."

"The first time you made love to me in that old copper bathtub I was certain we'd drown." Although she was a sophisticated woman of the 1990s, Jessica blushed at the memory of how daring she'd found his behavior.

Rory grinned as he recalled, with vivid accuracy, how they'd managed to not only flood the bathroom floor, but soak the kitchen ceiling below as well.

"I told you," he said, running his finger along the delicate top of the wondrously skimpy piece of lace that had replaced the boned corset that had been the fashion in his time, "the trick is to hold your breath."

"And I told you," she said, as his stroking touch made her knees weak, "that it's hard to breathe, period, whenever I'm around you."

"I know the feeling." He bent his head and his tongue made a wet swath along the flesh his finger had warmed. "Very well . . . So, how does this come off?"

"There's a hook. In front."

Jessica was not at all surprised when he found the front clasp and unfastened it without difficulty. Rory Mannion had always been a man who knew his way around women's clothing.

"Ah. That's better." His lips found the peak of her breast and teased it into rigid arousal.

"Much," she agreed, arching her back, inviting him to take her more fully into his mouth. Which he did, with pleasure. Fighting the need to rush, Rory moved his mouth to the other breast, teasing, tasting, savoring.

"I love this," he murmured as he unzipped her skirt and sent it skimming down over her hips.

"What?" She tried to remember that she'd wanted to undress him, but as so often happened when Rory made love to her, she couldn't think. Or breathe. Or move.

"Everything." He knelt down as he peeled the tights down her legs. "I love touching you."

He ran a finger up the inner flesh of her bare thigh, and was rewarded by Jessica's sharp intake of breath and her increased trembling. "I love tasting you." Rory kissed her quivering stomach, so enticingly bared by those skimpy panties. "I love the soft little sounds you make when I touch you, like this."

He cupped her throbbing feminine flesh with his palm and made her moan. The silk beneath his hand was hot and moist. Rory knew that she would be hotter. And wetter.

When he slipped a finger beneath the lace-trimmed edge, then delved into her heat, she tilted her head back, grabbed hold of his shoulders and tilted her hips toward him in a desperate, unspoken need for more.

"Rory." His name was torn from her throat on a desperate cry of need. "Please." His intimate touch was causing a painful, yet pleasurable tension inside her.

"There's no need to rush." He slipped another finger in and felt her body clutching desperately at him.

"That's what you think," she muttered, needing more. Needing him.

When she would have pulled away, he pressed his free hand against the base of her spine and held her tightly against his probing touch. When he felt her resistance ebb, he took his hand from her back and ripped away the panties with a single brisk stroke.

"You feel so good," he murmured as his fingers moved deep inside her, heating her from the inside out. And when he touched his mouth to that burning flesh, a violent tremor surged through her, and she cried out his name.

Rory thought the ragged voice reverberating off the walls was the sexiest thing he'd ever heard.

Her body was still rippling with convulsions as he half carried, half dragged her into the bathroom. He reached into the shower, turned on the water, then shed his own clothes with a speed that told her he was reaching the end of his amazing patience.

And then the warm water was sluicing over them, and he took the bar of French milled soap in his hands and worked it into a frothy white lather that he spread over her like a silken veil, making her swollen breasts glisten like precious jewels. He nibbled at the ultrasensitive nub between her legs with his teeth and brought her to yet another climax that left her shaking.

Needing to drive him as mad as he was driving her, she took the soap from his hands and spread it across his wide shoulders and down his chest, her fingernails scraping at the male nipples that turned as hard as dark brown stones beneath her sensuous touch.

Her palms moved over a stomach that she knew was rock hard from physical work rather than time spent with weights at some trendy 1990s gym. It was her turn to drop to her knees as she bathed each leg down to his feet, then moved back up again. His thighs were taut and muscled, and between them, a magnificent erection jutted boldly out from a nest of curly dark hair.

She stared, enthralled by the smooth length, the weight. How could she have forgotten this?

"I need you to touch me," he groaned.

Needing the same thing, she wrapped her fingers around him, loving the way she could feel his life force pulsing wildly beneath her touch. When she began to slowly stroke him, from base to deep purple tip, he leaned his head back against the tile, closed his eyes and thrust his hips toward her, exactly as she had done to him.

Emboldened, and remembering that sun-spangled day when she'd practically raped him after watching the circus performer swallow the gleaming sword all the way to its jeweled hilt, she took this man she knew to be her husband in her mouth, loving him with her lips, her tongue, her teeth.

"No." Gasping, he pulled away. "Not this time."

Loving the way he'd just assured her that there would be other times, that he wasn't going to disappear just when they'd finally found one another again, she granted his request, and kissed her way back up his wet torso, his throat, along his rigid jaw, until her avid mouth found his again.

The kiss was deep and hot. Tongues tangled as hearts entwined. And although Rory wanted to lift her up and lower her onto his aching shaft, he wasn't certain that his legs would hold them. So instead, he dragged her out of the shower, down onto the fluffy pink carpet.

Hunger burning through him, he spread her legs apart, not gently, then thrust into her, glistening wet marble into moist pink flesh. And although she was more than ready for him, she cried out in surprise and wonder at the way he filled her so completely.

He rose then surged back with a force that made her feel he could reach all the way to her throat. She wrapped her legs around his hips, raked her nails down his back as he rode her hard and fast until they were both shaken by a series of shattering orgasms that seemed to go on and on forever.

Jessica had no idea how long they lay there, surrounded by clouds of fragrant steam, arms and legs tangled, the water that had streamed off their bodies dampening the plush carpeting. She only knew that her heart was pounding with a force that couldn't possibly be normal for any human, its rhythm matching his, beat for every driving beat.

"I'm sorry." He lifted his head, brushed her wet hair away from her face and frowned down at her.

"I'm not." Although her arm felt strangely boneless and heavy at the same time, she managed to lift it enough that she could trace his tightly set lips with her finger. "I wanted you to make love to me, Rory."

"I wanted that, too, sweetheart." He pulled her closer, loving the little convulsions he could feel still rippling through her and around him. "But I wanted to do it right. I never intended to take you on the rug like some oversexed animal."

"You always were oversexed," she reminded him with a slow, satisfied smile. "That was one of the things I loved most about you."

"One of the things? What were the others?"

"I'm not certain I should tell you. Your ego is already immense. What if I cause it to grow even larger?"

"Talking about growing larger." He moved his hips as he swelled inside her again. "I want you again. But in a real bed. Where we can spend all night driving each other mad."

Jessica experienced a fleeting sense of loss as he pulled out of her and stood up, bringing her with him. He paused only long enough to turn off the water, which had turned ice-cold, then scooped her up, carried her into the bedroom and laid her on the four-poster bed. Then he made up for lost time by loving her all night long.

As the pink fingers of dawn rose over the treetops outside the house, Jessica fell into a deep, dreamless sleep, leaving Rory awake to look down into her face, her lovely, lovely face, and wonder what would happen to them after he killed Black Jack Clayton.

10

THE NEXT WEEK was like the honeymoon they'd never had. Although Jessica was disappointed when Monday came and she had to return to work, each night she'd return home to a home-cooked dinner and a husband who managed to remind her that sex wrapped in love was the most exquisite gift any two people could give to one another.

While she was at work, Rory spent much of his day reading and watching television, trying to catch up on the hundred years he'd missed. He was shocked by, yet attracted to, the steamy afternoon soaps. And he became a "Jeopardy" fan, although he couldn't understand why it was necessary to phrase answers in the form of questions.

But his favorite cable show was, hands down, "Court TV." Since he'd professed to have a degree from Harvard, she was not surprised to discover that he had a quick and brilliant mind. What did come as a revelation was how much she enjoyed discussing cases with him in the evening, and how his uncanny insight often aided her in planning her prosecution strategy. She remembered how, in their past life together, every so often he'd suggest a different view for one of her photographs, one she wouldn't have thought of.

At such times she'd told him that they made a great team. And after two weeks together, Jessica realized they still did.

"I don't know how I could have ever forgotten this," she said, as she sat amidst the love-rumpled sheets on the Wednesday evening before Thanksgiving, sipping the ruby cabernet sauvignon she'd brought home to accompany Rory's dinner.

He'd prepared beef stew because, he'd told her as he began unbuttoning her gold silk blouse before she'd even had an opportunity to put down her briefcase, it would hold until they'd satisfied other, more basic hungers.

"I think it's probably like Mac said," Rory mused. "All this is more difficult for the two of you, because of your spirits—or souls, or whatever—having come back in bodies that have experienced entirely different lives."

"I suppose." She sighed, thinking it was all too complex to try to unravel. "You and Mac seem to be becoming friends." She knew Rory had been spending a lot of time at the *Rim Rock Record* offices lately.

"He's been letting me go back through the newspaper morgue to learn about the changes in Whiskey River—and Arizona—over the past century. And, of course, we were close friends before, so it makes sense that we'd feel that connection."

"The same way you felt the instant antipathy toward Chapmann?" Neither of them had spoken of Chapmann since the first night they'd made love. But the thought of him had been hovering over them nevertheless, like a black storm cloud hovering on the horizon.

Rory heard the question in her voice and knew that she wanted reassurance that he wouldn't do anything to harm the man he believed had killed them both a century ago. But as much as he would have loved to be able to tell her what she needed to hear, he loved her too much ever to lie to her.

"Let's not talk about Clayton." He reached over and topped off her wineglass. "We'll have a little more wine, make love again, then I'll dish up the best stew you've ever eaten."

She laughed at that. "Pretty sure of yourself, aren't you?"

"About what?" He cocked a devilish brow. "Are you referring to my ability to rise to the occasion again, so to speak? Or my culinary prowess?"

Even the way he looked at her, with that combination of tenderness and lust, was enough to arouse her. Without taking her eyes from his, she drained her wineglass, then put it on the bedside table.

"I'd never doubt anything about you," she said honestly as she twined her arms around his neck and touched her lips to his. "But this time I want to make love to you."

His pleased laugh was a warm breeze against her smiling mouth. And as he allowed her to pull him back down onto the mattress, Rory could not think of a single solitary objection.

THE PRESCOTT RANCH proved that time definitely moved slower in this part of the country. The land, with its rolling meadows and forested acres, was much as Rory remembered it. Although the house boasted a wing that hadn't been there a hundred years ago, not much more had changed. The antique furniture would have been new in his time, and Rory remembered the heavy trestle dining table well from times he'd been invited to dinner in what he'd come to think of as his former life.

The food was delicious and there was an amazing amount of it, although Rory found the domestically raised turkey bland compared to the wild ones he remembered. The company was enjoyable and although he could tell that Trace was still withholding judgment on him, Mariah Swann Callahan had welcomed him into her family home with a genuine warmth that he knew was not feigned.

The conversation flowed as easily as the wine and Rory was relieved when his presence was accepted without undue question.

"Your friends are nice people," he said to Jessica as they drove back to her house after dinner.

Mariah had insisted on sending home enough leftovers to feed an army. The aromas of sweet potatoes, turkey and sausage dressing mingled with that of pumpkin pie and Jess's perfume in the warmth of the car.

"They are, aren't they?" she agreed. "When Trace first started falling in love with Mariah, I have to admit I was a little worried."

"Because you thought she might have killed her sister to get the ranch?" Greed, Rory knew, was a powerful motive for murder, in any century.

"No, although Trace was forced to suspect everyone, including Mariah, I never believed she had anything to do with Laura's death. What worried me was my original belief that a hotshot screenwriter would become bored stiff here in Whiskey River. But, amazingly, she seems to be thriving."

"She looked very happy," he agreed. "But of course, the fact that she's going to be a mother may have had something to do with that."

"I'm so happy for them." Mariah had announced her news at dinner, to the delight of everyone present. "I don't think I've ever seen Trace look so damn proud of himself."

"He was entitled. After all, now he's assured that his line will continue."

"Is that important to you?" she asked with a great deal more casualness than she felt.

Rory was vaguely disappointed that she'd obviously forgotten that she'd once professed a desire for a large family. "Of course. I think it is for most men."

"I don't know about most men. But I do think Mariah's pregnancy will probably be rough on Clint."

"He's the rancher who was supposed to come to dinner and didn't?"

"That's him." The afternoon drizzle was beginning to turn to wet snow that was hitting the windshield in thick white splats. She turned up her wipers and clicked the lights to high beams. "He owns the land next door. He was also madly in love with Laura."

Rory watched the light cut through the falling snow and for not the first time since his adventure had begun, wondered if the people of this time had any idea how fortunate they were to have so many wondrous inventions.

"I suppose he didn't feel inclined to make casual dinner party conversation."

"You're probably right." Jessica sighed, thinking back on the case. "It's strange how life turns out. If Laura hadn't been murdered, Trace and Mariah probably wouldn't have fallen in love and wouldn't be planning for their child. But on the other hand, Laura and Clint would be living in the Prescott ranch house, fixing up the nursery for the baby Laura was expecting."

Rory thought about that and considered how fate was, indeed, a strange and fickle mistress. "It was Clint's child? Not her husband's?"

"DNA tests proved it was Clint's."

Rory thought about that as well, put himself into the rancher's place and wondered how the man had the strength to go on. "He lost a great deal."

"Yes." Jessica's voice was low and sad. "More than any man should have to, and he hasn't dealt with it very well. I worry about him."

A recent memory flashed through Rory's mind. Of Jessica's hand pressed against a man's rugged cheek. Of her expression of concern as she'd looked up into that bleak face.

"He's the man outside the pharmacy."

"What?" She glanced over at him, clearly surprised.

"The day I saw Chapmann for the first time. Right before you entered the pharmacy, you stopped to talk to a man who'd just come out. I remember thinking at the time you seemed close."

"I suppose we are. Although I didn't even know him until I nearly prosecuted him for Laura's murder, I've come to care a great deal for him."

She shook her head. "Everyone in town likes and respects Clint. Mariah, who's known him since she was a child, is the closest to him of any of us who were at the ranch today. But we were all hoping he'd come to dinner."

"It's hard to lose someone you love," Rory said softly.

Jessica slanted another, longer look at him. "Yes. But sometimes people find each other again."

"I liked Gavin Thomas," Rory said, wanting to change the bittersweet mood.

"Oh, so do I," Jessica agreed quickly. "I don't know all the details, but he and Trace grew up together in Dallas, which is why he moved here."

"It's quite a coincidence that he's creating a new series of graphic novels featuring a time-traveling old-time western marshall."

"I just about choked on my wine when he dropped that little bombshell. And you're right, it's an amazing coincidence. Are you going to help him with his research?"

Since Rory's presence was difficult to explain, they'd decided to simply introduce him as a western historian. Jessica had been more than a little relieved when Trace, who was still irritated about his inability to locate Rory Mannion on any of the national-search computer networks, hadn't blown their cover.

"I may as well. If some of the movies I've been watching on television are any indication, there's a great deal of misinformation written about my time. I suppose I have some responsibility to set the record straight."

"I wouldn't hold your breath waiting for that to happen," Jessica warned him. "I remember when Gavin first came to town, Brigid Delaney—Tara Delaney's grandmother—wasn't at all pleased with his current heroine."

"The crime-fighting witch he was telling me about."

"Morganna, Mistress of the Night," Jessica agreed. "Personally, if I'd been Brigid, I would have hit the roof at the way he depicted witches as vengeful sex objects. But being a kindhearted, not to mention broad-minded soul, she calmly set out to reeducate him instead."

"Reeducate him? About witches?"

"Exactly."

"Surely you're not saying that the charming woman I met today had a witch for a grandmother?"

"What's the matter? Don't you believe in witches?"

"Of course not." He folded his arms over the front of his chest. "The very idea is preposterous."

"Most people would probably say the same thing about time travel," Jessica said dryly.

"Point taken." Rory thought about that for a while. "You know," he said, "if Brigid Delaney really was a witch, that could explain why her granddaughter responded so strangely to me."

"Tara responded strangely? How?"

"When we shook hands, her eyes suddenly grew wider and she looked shocked and quite shaken. Actually," he said, "now that I think about it, it reminded me a great deal of how Noel reacted at first."

It was Jessica's turn to be quiet as she pondered the idea. "It's possible, I suppose. As crazy as it may seem to outsiders, a lot of people in Whiskey River believed in Brigid's supposed Druidic powers. If Tara inherited any of her grandmother's talents, she could have sensed something."

"I think that was undoubtedly what happened." Rory rubbed his jaw, which only bore one nick today. He was definitely getting the hang of that thin little pink razor. As he'd proven when he'd shaved Jess's long legs last night while they'd taken a bath together. "Whiskey River is truly a remarkable place."

"It is that." Jessica shared his amazement at not only their own situation, but Mac's and Noel's. And now she was forced to wonder about Tara Delaney, as well. "Perhaps Noel was right, after all."

He glanced over at her. "About what?"

"About Whiskey River being like Brigadoon, just waiting for us all to find it."

"It's a pleasant thought."

"Isn't it? Perhaps it'll be Clint's turn next," she suggested with a smile.

"Are you suggesting that his Laura will come back?"

"Wouldn't that be wonderful? Or, barring that, perhaps his guardian angel will land in town."

"Or his fairy godmother."

"Clint in a pumpkin coach?" Jessica shook her head. "I think that's a bit farfetched, even for Whiskey River."

They shared a laugh, enjoying the day. And each other.

IN A SHADED grove where Whiskey River widened into a deep pool, Rory and Jessica were making love. She was down to those skimpy lace confections that he'd decided were definitely one of the very best things about the twentieth century. Her flesh gleamed golden in the buttery rays of sunshine slanting down through the treetops. Her eyes sparkled with a gilt-edged feminine invitation no man in his right mind would be able to ignore, even if he wanted to. Which Rory most definitely didn't.

"You are so beautiful." He skimmed his lips down her throat, pausing to touch the tip of his tongue against her thudding pulse. "So luscious." His lips continued their sensual journey, dampening the shell-pink lace of her bra. "Sometimes I can't believe that you're mine."

She arched her back off the blanket he'd spread atop the soft natural bed of pine needles. "I've always been yours," she murmured, combing her hands through his hair, pressing him more deeply into flesh heated by sun and desire. The scent on her warm skin filled the air around them, making Rory feel as if they were making love in a tropical garden. "I'll always be yours. Forever."

She could not have said anything that would have pleased him more. And although when he'd first brought her here he'd planned to make love to her slowly and tenderly, her murmured words made hunger flare up from some primal dark pit inside him.

He was overcome with a hot need to claim her, to brand her for all eternity as his own. Her panties had little ribbon bows at the hips. Rory ripped one of the ties, giving his mouth access to the moist pink lips between her thighs, and feasted hungrily, when suddenly a siren's scream shattered the erotic mood.

"What the hell?" He sat bolt upright in bed and immediately began to cough.

"It's the smoke detector," Jessica, who'd been jerked from a deep sleep as well, said. "Oh, my God, the house is on fire!"

Fire. Rory's first thought was self-directed fury that he'd allowed his love for Jess and his happiness at finding his bride again, to detract him from his plan to avenge Emilie's murder.

By letting his head be ruled by his heart, he'd made a disastrous mistake. A mistake that could prove to be fatal.

No! This time Clayton wasn't going to get away with murder. And this time Rory was going to save his wife's life.

He was out of bed in a flash, scooping up the clothes that Jessica had dropped carelessly onto the floor as she'd undressed him with slow hands that had succeeded in turning his body to flame.

"We've got to get out of here," he said as he jerked on his jeans. She should have been beside him, gathering up her own clothes. But instead, she sat in the middle of the bed, unmoving, as if carved from stone. Her eyes were wide with fear, her hands were holding the sheet in a death grip.

Hell. How could he have forgotten Jess's fear of fire?

"Jess." He took hold of her right hand and tried to loosen her stiff fingers. "We have to get out of here, now."

"It's no use." Her voice sounded so very far away, as if it were coming from inside a cave. As she looked up at him, her bleak gaze reminded him of a woman who'd visited hell and had lived to tell about it. "We can't get out. He's bolted the doors."

The smoke was getting thicker by the moment. Rory wondered if it was his imagination, fired by that century-old scene he'd been forced to witness right before Clayton had shot him, or whether the sounds of flames crackling on the floor below were real.

Although he wanted to yell at her to get out now, he forced his voice into one of reassuring calm. "That was then." He managed, with considerable effort, to release her hold on the sheet long enough to slip his shirt onto her. "These are different times, darlin'." With fingers that felt like stone, he buttoned the shirt as far as her waist. "You're not alone this time."

He tried to lift her from the mattress, but she was so stiff she felt like deadweight in his arms. "I'm with you. I'll get us out of here." He leaned down and gave her a deep kiss designed to reassure her. And, hopefully, get her mind off her terror.

"Rory?" Her lips were trembling as she looked up at him.

"It's me, sweetheart." He kissed her again. Harder, deeper.

"You've come home?"

For a moment the words caught him off guard. Then, looking down into those wide terrified eyes, he realized that she was no longer Jess, but Emilie.

"I've come home." He ran his hands over her shoulders, soothing the tense muscles. "Just in time to get you out of here, Em."

And then she did something that surprised him. She smiled. A slow, soft, trusting smile that tore at every fiber of his being.

"I knew you'd come." As compliant as a baby lamb, she held out her hand and let him lead her out of the bed, across the room, and into the bathroom, where he wet two washcloths in the sink.

"Hold this over your mouth and nose." He handed her one of the lace-trimmed cloths, then grabbed up his gun, which Trace had returned after he was convinced that Rory hadn't stolen it. He stuck the revolver into his waistband. "And get down on your knees. The air is fresher closer to the floor."

Without a word of argument, she did as instructed, and crawling on her hands and knees, followed him down the narrow hallway.

"Hell." Rory let out a string of frustrated, vicious curses when they found the downstairs engulfed in flames.

"That's all right." She treated him to another sweet smile and although the way she seemed to have drifted off into her own safe little world made goose bumps rise on Rory's arms, he supposed he should be grateful that she no longer seemed to be fully cognizant of the danger they were in. "You'll get us out. I trust you Rory, darling."

With her life. She didn't say it, but both of them understood that was exactly what she was doing. Rory knew that if he lived another thousand lifetimes, he'd never forgive himself for not arriving home soon enough to save his bride from a horrific death. He was not about to face eternity with two such failures on his conscience.

"We'll have to go back to the bedroom and jump," he decided. They'd undoubtedly break a few bones, but that was definitely better than the alternative.

"We won't have to jump."

There was a sudden roar as the flames engulfed the stairway, swallowing it whole like a hungry dragon.

"Honey, we don't have any choice."

"We can use the ladder."

"The ladder?"

She took the washcloth from her mouth long enough for him to see a smile that was so quick and so self-satisfied that Rory realized that somehow Jess had come back just in time to do what Emilie couldn't.

"There's a rope ladder under the bed. I saw it last month in a catalog and it seemed like a good idea. So I ordered it."

Fate, Rory thought for not the first time since landing in Whiskey River in 1996, was definitely an amazing thing. He framed her face with his hands and gave her another quick hot kiss. "I love you."

They made their way back down the hall, and into the smoke-filled bedroom, where Rory closed the door behind them. While he got the rope ladder out from beneath the bed, Jess ran into the bathroom and soaked a towel in water and put it against the bottom of the door.

"It might slow the fire down," she said. "And it should stop the smoke long enough for us to get out of here."

The ladder had hooks that fit over the window sash. Rory got it in place, leaned out, and tugged. "I think it's secure."

"If it isn't, the worst that can happen is we fall," she stated with the attorney's logic he'd come to admire.

"And that definitely beats staying here and becoming a crispy critter."

As they climbed out the window, Jess first, Rory right behind her, they heard the sound of sirens in the distance. Right before he reached the safety of the ground, Rory saw the flashing red lights coming their way from town. And he saw something else, too: a pair of tail-lights, gleaming red in the dark, driving away from the house.

Obviously Clayton was up to his old tricks. On the ground, from a safe distance, Rory took Jessica into his arms, and held her tightly as they watched the roof of her beloved Cape Cod house fall in with a roar and a crash that sent sparks flying up into the midnight black sky, and vowed that this time Black Jack Clayton wasn't going to get away.

"YOU JUST DON'T get it, do you?"

A very frustrated Trace was pacing the floor of his den. He'd brought Jessica and the man who continued to insist his name was Rory Mannion back to the ranch after the fire. Fortunately, he and Rory wore the same size clothes, and while Jessica was a bit taller than Mariah, the difference wasn't enough to matter. Although the fire department wouldn't be able to sift through the ashes until morning, it had been obvious that the house—and everything in it—was going to be a total loss.

"There is no way in hell I'm going to let you go after Chapmann."

"He tried to kill Jess," Rory reminded the sheriff. "Someone has to bring him to justice."

"If he is the one who did it—" Trace held up a hand to forestall Rory's interruption "—and while I tend to agree with you that he probably was, it's my job, as sheriff of Mogollon County, to be the one to arrest him."

"It's going to take more than one man."

"Fine. I've got deputies. And I can call in DPS to watch the highways."

"He won't be on the highways. He's going to head into the woods."

"It's beginning to snow again. The temperature's dropped into the teens. If he is out there, he's going to be freezing his tail off before morning. We'll flush him out."

"It's not going to be as easy as you're suggesting," Rory insisted. "The man grew up here, he knows every rock and tree, every nook and cranny and cave. He could hide out for weeks."

"Not in this weather."

Rory cursed. "You don't know him like I do."

"You've only been in town, what? Two and a half weeks? And part of that time you were unconscious. I don't think that makes you an expert on Eric Chapmann."

"No. But I am an expert on Jack Clayton."

"Dammit, would you knock it off about Clayton?" Trace roared, losing what little patience he had left.

Jessica was in Mariah and Trace's bedroom, changing into a pair of silk pajamas and a heavy robe that should have warmed her, but didn't. Her blood still felt like ice in her veins, a feeling that had little to do with the time she'd spent standing outside her house in the freezing sleet.

"It's not like Trace to yell," she murmured.

"No," Mariah agreed. "The last time I heard him bellow like that was after he found out I'd broken into Alan's hotel room looking for proof he'd killed Laura."

"He was worried about you."

"True."

Mariah remembered that the fight had ended with Trace hovering over her as she lay on her back on the floor, proving without a single doubt that she hadn't gotten her money's worth from that self-defense course she'd taken from the high-priced Beverly Hills jujitsu expert. His fury had soon dissipated, replaced with something even darker, more primitive. More exciting.

When she felt her lips curving into a reminiscent smile, she chided herself for forgetting that a woman who'd come to be her friend had nearly lost her life tonight.

"And now he's worried about you."

"He takes too much on his shoulders."

Mariah shrugged, knowing, better than most, how futile it was to try to change nature. "Trace has wide shoulders. So does Rory."

"Yes." Jessica sighed. A significant little silence settled over the room.

Mariah sat down on the edge of the king-size bed and patted the mattress. "Want to talk about it?"

Jessica stared out into the well of darkness, and although she knew it was merely her imagination working overtime, for a fleeting instant the sight of her house going up in flames flickered through her mind.

She knew, without a doubt, that she would have died if Rory hadn't been in bed with her tonight. When the smoke detector had jerked her from her sleep, she'd been literally paralyzed with that primal, instinctive fear of fire she'd lived with all of her life. She knew she would not have been able to move had it not been for her absolute trust in Rory.

"It's difficult," she murmured, wondering what Mariah would say if she told her that the man who'd saved her life tonight was her husband from another time.

"Love usually is. Lord knows, Trace and I didn't exactly have an easy time of it."

"Your circumstances were unusual. After all, you met the morning of your sister's murder. Trace had to consider you a suspect and at the same time you were worried he'd cave in to pressure from your father—not to mention the national media—to solve the case quickly."

"I think I knew right off the bat he wouldn't do that," Mariah admitted.

"Oh?" Jessica was surprised. "Trace told me you accused him of being one of the stereotypical corrupt rubes you routinely wrote into your television crime show scripts."

Mariah smiled and blushed at the same time. "I didn't exactly say that," she corrected, "but I suppose I did imply it. But then, when he laid down the law to me, and wouldn't cave in to my own methods of persuasion, I knew he was a straight arrow."

"I assume your methods were not without their appeal."

Mariah Swann Callahan was the most naturally sexy woman Jessica had ever known. Even now, wearing one of Trace's oversize T-shirts over the top of a pair of prison gray, waffle-weave sweatpants, and with her hair uncombed, she managed to look like the kind of woman for which satin sheets and French champagne had been invented.

Despite the seriousness of the reason Jessica was here in her bedroom in the middle of the night, Mariah laughed. "They didn't call me the Vixen of Whiskey River for nothing." Her expression sobered as she looked up at Jessica. "Do you remember that night we went out to dinner together in Payson?"

"Of course." Mariah had almost been killed that night. Just as she'd almost died tonight. The idea made Jessica shiver.

"You assured me that what you and Trace had wasn't serious," Mariah reminded her. "That it couldn't be serious, because he was too strong willed. You said you could only be happy with the kind of man who'd let you wear the pants in the family."

"That's what I always believed." Jessica dragged her hand through her hair and smelled smoke. "But that was before I met Rory."

"Funny how the right man can change a woman's plans," Mariah said dryly. "And a man's. Looks as if Whiskey River has just gotten a new historian."

The casual, encouraging remark brought up the question Jessica'd been asking herself for days. The all-important question she and Rory had been avoiding.

"I don't know if he'll be staying." Her tone was flat and discouraged.

"Of course he will." Mariah leaned over and gave her a friendly hug. "I've seen the way he looks at you. The man's obviously head over heels in love with you, Jess. There's no earthly power that could get him to walk away from that."

That, Jessica knew, was true. But once again she was forced to wonder what Mariah would say about the unearthly powers in Whiskey River, powers beyond anyone's control.

11

WHILE MARIAH and Jessica were sharing womanly secrets Rory continued to argue with Trace.

"There's one thing you need to understand," he said. "I'm going after Clayton. With or without your approval. And there's not a damn thing you can do to stop me."

Trace looked every bit as frustrated as Rory felt. "I can lock you up in jail. And throw the key in Whiskey River."

"Not legally." Even in Rory's time, although the parameters were admittedly stretched in the Wild West, unlawful arrest was officially discouraged.

"I have a rule about civilians mucking around in a case," Trace argued. "Especially one that could involve violence."

"And yet, Jessica tells me that you break that rule on occasion. Such as when you allowed Mariah to assist you with her sister's murder investigation."

"It wasn't as if I had much choice," Trace muttered. "She also ended up almost getting killed, which proves my point."

"You don't have any choice this time, either. And I have no intention of getting killed."

"That's what they all say," Trace muttered.

"There is a way to compromise."

"*Compromise* has never been one of my favorite words. But what do you suggest?"

"You could always deputize me."

Trace stared at him. "Now I know you're crazy."

"It's not impossible. There are many cases of modern day civilian posses. Even here in Arizona. I read in the paper of a group of ordinary citizens in Phoenix who have formed patrols—"

"Not in my county," Trace interjected. "And not to go after would-be murderers."

"Perhaps you're forgetting that I was one of the people Chapmann tried to murder. But more importantly, he tried to kill Jess. And there is no way in hell that I'm going to let him get away with that."

Trace cursed and shook his head.

"How would you feel," Rory continued, pressing his case, "if it had been Mariah who'd nearly been burned alive?"

"I'd want to kill the black-hearted son of a bitch." Trace's tone was flat. And final.

"Exactly."

The two men stared at each other. Finally Trace cursed again. "All right. But if I deputize you, you're going to have to follow my orders."

"Of course," Rory agreed quickly.

Too quickly, Trace thought, already regretting his decision.

Jessica was even more concerned by the idea of Rory going after Eric Chapmann than Trace. "You can't possibly be serious," she said, after he'd come into the bedroom to share his plans. Mariah had taken one look at Rory's grim face and left them alone.

"You know that I am."

"It's Trace's job to bring him in."

"Legally." He ran his hands down her arms and linked their fingers together. "Morally, it's mine."

"But the last time—"

"The last time I made the mistake of leaving you unprotected. Trace is getting an officer from the state police to come guard you and Mariah while we're gone. You'll be well protected."

"Still, what if he ambushes you?" *As he did before.* The words hovered unspoken between them.

"If that happens, we're obviously in some sort of weird time loop," he decided. "Which means you'll come along and rescue me again."

Jessica didn't know whether to laugh or to cry at his bad joke. "Don't you take anything seriously?"

"Of course." He drew her into his arms and held her close. "I take Clayton seriously." He pressed his lips against the top of her head, breathing in the scent of smoke in her hair. It had been so close, Rory thought darkly. Too close. His caressing hands skimmed her ribs, teased her breasts, cradled her hips. "And most important, I take my feelings for you very, very seriously."

She tilted her head back to look up at him. Tears glistened wetly in her eyes, her lips managed a trembling smile. "I love you. So much. If anything happened to you . . ."

"Nothing's going to happen." He bent his head and kissed her, eyes open and on hers. "I swear, as soon as I make certain that Clayton is out of our lives, once and for all, I'll come back to you."

His lips nibbled leisurely at hers, as if they had all the time in the world, as if Trace wasn't in the other room waiting for him.

"And we'll get married again, and live to a ripe old age, watching our grandchildren ride horses and run wild in the woods. And years from now, Mac will run the announcement of our fiftieth wedding anniversary in the *Rim Rock Record*, and people will ask us the secret for staying married for half a century and we'll tell them that the secret to a successful marriage is a deep and all-abiding love."

His tantalizing kisses, his stroking hands, his warm, reassuring words spun a shimmering web around Jessica, seducing her into submission.

"And," he added as her lips softened beneath his and her arms crept up his chest to wrap around his neck, "of course it helps to be lucky enough to be married to the sexiest woman on the face of the earth."

She knew he'd wanted to make her laugh, but instead, his attempt at humor only made her realize exactly how much she'd lose if anything happened to him.

She wasn't going to panic, because it wouldn't help. And she wasn't going to cry because it would only make him feel guilty, and if he was worried about her, he might allow his mind to drift at the wrong moment, giving Clayton the upper hand.

What she was going to do, she realized, was let Rory live out his destiny. She took a deep breath to keep the tears at bay.

"Whatever happens," she said on a voice choked with emotion, "remember that I love you. More than life itself."

There was hunger in her avid kiss. Hunger, desperation and urgency. Rory could taste it as her tongue tangled with his, could feel it as molten heat radiated from her body, could hear it in the primitive sounds torn from her throat. His own blood, fired by her desperate passion, thundered in his ears, seeming to call out her name over and over again.

Emilie. Jess. Emilie. The two women had become intrinsically linked in his mind and in his heart. And he loved them both. For all time.

It took every ounce of inner resolve Rory possessed to finally break off the heated kiss. He framed her face in his hands. "I have to go. But I promise I'll be back before you know it. Safe and sound."

He'd said those same words to her before, Jess knew. And, amazingly, although he'd been a century late, he had come back. She could only hope she wouldn't have to wait another hundred years to see the only man she'd ever loved—the only man she could ever love—again.

He kissed her one more time, a swift hot kiss that did nothing to ease the pain, then released her and walked out of the room to join Trace in his search for Black Jack Clayton alias Eric Chapmann.

The DPS officer who'd arrived while Rory had been talking with Jessica objected to the two women standing in the open doorway, but there was no way he was going to keep them from watching their men set off on their mission.

"They'll be back," Mariah assured Jessica as they watched the Suburban's taillights disappear into the swirling white snow.

Tears streaming down her face, Jessica couldn't answer. All she could do now was to wait. And pray.

"I STILL DON'T get it," Trace said as he drove the Suburban high into the mountains. The abandoned forest service road was little more than a series of rocks followed by potholes deep enough to bury the tires nearly up to the rims. Behind them, the two-horse trailer bounced along.

"What makes you think Chapmann's up here? The logical thing is for him to have taken off to one of the cities—Phoenix, Tucson, or even Denver—where he could blend in."

"And the police are looking for him in all those cities," Rory said. "But the kind of man who'd set fires to kill people isn't logical. You can't use routine police procedures to track him down."

What Rory could not tell Trace was that Wolfe had once shown him the cave he and Noel had camped out in while they'd been on the run from Black Jack and the posse that had been pursing them. Later, when he'd gone searching for the killer himself, he'd found evidence that Clayton had camped out in the cave. Unfortunately, after luring Rory away from Whiskey River—and his bride—the outlaw had doubled back to town.

The sun had come up, gleaming blindingly through the tops of the shaggy, white-draped pine trees, making the freshly fallen snow sparkle like diamonds. It was a pristine, deceptively peaceful scene. It was hard to believe the evil that was lurking not far away.

"Well, guess we've hit the end of the road." Trace frowned at the huge boulder blocking the way. "Time to play cowboys and bad guys."

They left the Suburban and walked back to the trailer. The horses were sturdy and surefooted. As he pulled himself astride the mare, Rory felt instantly at home. Although there was a great deal to be said for automobiles—he certainly enjoyed driving Jess's Jaguar—there was still nothing like a good horse.

They rode in silence, single file, through the canyon cut by Whiskey River over the aeons. Little puffs of breath like ghosts rose from his mare's nostrils. The day was so clear and cold he could see the crystals dancing in the air. The only sound was the clop of the horses' hooves on the rocky ground.

"How much further?" Trace asked from behind Rory. Although they'd experienced a brief argument over who would go first, Rory had finally convinced the sheriff that since he was the one who knew the cave's location, he should lead the way.

"It's not far." At least Rory didn't think it was. Although he recognized some of the landmarks, others had disappeared over the years.

"Good. Because I'm about to freeze my ass off."

Rory secretly shared Trace's discomfort. There'd once been a time when he never would have thought of complaining, not even to himself. Obviously modern conveniences like car heaters softened a man.

He was about to voice that opinion when a shot rang out, the report echoing all around them in the high canyon walls. Rory heard Trace's curse.

Both men dived to the ground, and the frightened horses took off at a gallop. "Did he hit you?" Rory asked as he and Trace ducked for cover.

"In the arm," Trace muttered as he glared down at the hole in the sleeve of the new leather jacket Mariah had given him for his birthday the previous week. Hell, he ought to shoot Chapmann just for this. "It's not that bad." Another shot whizzed by, ricocheted off a nearby tree trunk and sent splinters of bark flying.

Rory noted that Trace had managed to take his rifle with him when he'd dived off his gelding. Instincts like that were to be admired. Especially in this day and age when such shoot-outs were obviously not the norm.

"Where the hell is he?" Trace demanded. He glared up at the rocky escarpment.

The answer came in another volley of shots.

"Up there," Rory said, pointing to a huge red boulder the size of Trace's Suburban. "If you can hold him there, I'll try to climb up behind him."

"That's my job."

"You have the rifle," Rory pointed out. "I have the revolver. It makes more sense for you to keep him occupied while I do the close-up work."

"Hell, you just want to kill him."

"Hell yes," Rory nearly shouted back. "And in case you haven't noticed, he's doing his damnedest to kill us. Just keep him shooting," he repeated. "There used to be a trail not far from here, cut by elk coming down to the river. With any luck, it'll still be there. I'll climb up and jump him while you draw his fire."

"I feel like an extra in a Roy Rogers movie," Trace grumbled. "Or the remake of the shoot-out at O.K. Corral. This is ridiculous."

"It can also be deadly," Rory reminded him. "And it's definitely no movie." As if to underscore his words, a bullet hit a tree inches from his head.

"You don't have to convince me." Trace sighted the rifle, lined up his shot and pulled the trigger. He looked over at Rory's pearl-handled revolver. "Does that thing even work?"

"Of course. At least it did the last time I fired it." He decided this was not the time to reveal exactly how many years ago that had been.

"Where the hell is the SWAT team when you need them?" Trace growled as another shot sang by them.

Missed again. Clayton never was that good a shot, Rory remembered. Which was why he tended to limit his victims to innocent homesteaders who couldn't fight back.

Fortunately, the trail was there, just as he remembered, just as it had been a century ago. Rory silently thanked the elk for not having altered their pattern over the years. He climbed nearly silently, watching where he walked, being careful not to step on dry twigs or dislodge rocks as Wolfe had taught him. The sound of gunfire continued.

He reached the top of the cliff. Clayton was crouched behind a boulder, his attention directed down into the canyon. It would be so easy to shoot him in the back. And even if there were questions, he figured the fact that the outlaw had already shot the sheriff would justify such an action.

He pulled his gun from his waistband, aimed and couldn't fire. He wanted to kill Clayton, but not this way. The biggest difference between him and Black Jack Clayton, Rory realized, was that although he had regrettably killed other men, he'd never drawn first. And never in cold blood.

"It's over, Clayton," he said. His voice was quiet, but easily heard in the stillness of the canyon.

The man spun around and leaped to his feet in one quick movement. The barrel of his rifle was pointed directly at Rory's chest. His torn jeans and the amount of blood flowing down his left leg from his inner thigh revealed that at least one of Trace's shots had hit home.

The wound, which looked painful and potentially deadly, did not seem to encourage the outlaw's surrender.

"You're right, Mannion," he growled. His malevolent gaze told Rory that at that moment, he knew exactly who Rory was. "It's over. For you. I should have hung around to make sure I killed you the first time. When you came back and found your sweet little bride being barbecued in her cute little blue house."

Fury surged. Knowing that Clayton was trying to rattle him, Rory forced himself to remain calm. "You're not going to get away this time."

Clayton roared with amusement at that idea. "Wrong again, lawman." His evil grin belonged on the face of Death himself as he pulled the trigger.

A roar echoed around them. Birds took to the air, squirrels screeched and chattered in fear. There was a singing sound as the bullet hit a rock inches from Rory.

Although time seemed to have slowed to a snail's pace, Rory knew that only an instant had passed since Clayton had pulled the trigger.

He slowly, carefully, pulled the trigger of the .45 that had served him so long and so well.

The shot hit Clayton in the chest. His eyes widened in shock. His face twisted in anguish.

And then Rory watched as the man he'd sworn either to capture or kill fell over the edge of the Mogollon Rim to his death.

DESPITE THE ICY weather, Jessica paced the porch of the old Prescott ranch house, her arms wrapped around herself more for comfort than warmth. Where was Rory? He and Trace had been gone for hours.

"Clayton couldn't have killed him," she assured herself. "It wouldn't be fair. Surely fate didn't bring us together after all these years only to separate us again?"

Jessica told herself that. Over and over again. But the words did nothing to soothe her turmoiled mind. So she kept pacing.

Just when she thought her nerves were going to jump out of her chilled skin, Jessica saw the Suburban driving up the curving road to the house. And although the logical part of her mind knew it was impossible, she would have sworn her heart stopped.

The passenger door opened. And then she saw him. Safe, alive, walking toward her.

Weeping and laughing at the same time, she ran down the porch steps and flung herself joyously into Rory's arms.

"WHERE DO YOU think he is?" Jessica whispered as she and Rory lay together in the wide bed in Mariah and Trace's guest room.

"In hell," he whispered back against her hair. "Counting the wages of sin."

Jessica shivered at the mental image his words created. "I was so worried."

"You shouldn't have been. I told you I'd be back."

"I know." Still trembling, she wrapped her arms more tightly around him. "But you told me that once before."

"And I did return." He began unbuttoning the silk pajama top Mariah had lent her.

The touch of his hands on her flesh was like a brand, claiming her for all time. When she was struck with a sudden urge to cry, Jessica swallowed back the sob and tried to forget her fears and concentrate on the pleasure.

"Ah, but you forgot to tell me it was going to take you a hundred years."

"My mistake." He cupped her breasts, his thumbs teasing her nipples into taut peaks. "Next time I promise not to stay away so long."

He lowered his head and took one of those rosy crests between his lips and began sucking in a way that created an exquisite pull between her legs. She wanted to cry out, but knowing that Trace and Mariah were just across the hall, she instead buried her mouth into his shoulder.

"Something else worried me," she admitted, still whispering. "I was afraid that after you killed Black Jack, that once you'd gotten your revenge, you'd be gone. Back to your own time, like what happened to Noel after she saved Wolfe."

He'd worried about that as well. "Obviously, fate has other plans in store for us," he murmured, switching to the other breast. "Like this."

He took his time, treating each breast to a sensual assault that went on and on until she was writhing beneath him, desperate for more.

"Not yet."

Although he'd never admit it to her, Rory was panic-stricken that once they'd made love he'd be pulled back into his own time, forced to leave Jess behind. And he couldn't bear the prospect of losing her again.

So, although as always when he was with her, he felt as explosive as gunpowder, instead of taking her in a whirlwind of passion as he so often did, Rory forced himself to take his time.

It had never been like this. Jessica lay naked on the bed, the borrowed pajamas stripped off her an eternity ago. Her eyes were closed, her breath was weak and shallow. She was his for the taking. And oh, dear heaven, how he took!

His mouth skimmed over her moist flesh and she burned. His fingers tangled in the damp curls between her thighs, probing for feminine secrets, and liquid heat flowed forth like warm honey. Never had she been so aware of her body. He touched her wherever he chose, tasted wherever he wanted until she was certain that not a single inch of flaming skin had gone unloved. She couldn't count the number of times she'd come; her climaxes seemed to be as endless as their love.

She'd never known passion could be so unbearably sweet. Or pleasure so strong. He'd imprisoned her in a world of mist and smoke and warmth and she didn't ever want to escape.

"Lord, I love you like this," he murmured against her throat as he lifted her hips and slid into the welcoming warmth that so generously enfolded him. "Warm, willing, all mine."

"Yours," she managed to whisper. She lifted arms that seemed remarkably heavy to spread her fingers on his back and urge him closer. And together, they discovered paradise on earth.

JESSICA HAD NO idea how long she'd been asleep. But the sun was slipping through the crack in the draperies when she finally opened her eyes to find Rory, propped up on one elbow, gazing down at her.

"You're still here." Relief shimmered in her eyes.

"I'm still here." He'd been feeling the same relief for hours as he'd watched her sleep.

She pressed a trembling hand against his cheek. "When you didn't leave after killing Clayton, I thought that perhaps, after we'd made love one more time . . ."

"I know." He turned his head and kissed her palm. "I was worried about the same thing. But it seems, my love, that you're stuck with me."

"I can't think of anyone I'd rather be stuck with." Jessica laughed, unable to remember ever having been this happy. In either lifetime. "And, don't forget, it works both ways. You're stuck with me, too."

Their fingers linked, their eyes met, their hearts entwined. Then they smiled.

"Eternally," they said together.

MEN OF WHISKEY RIVER

**Three sexy, unforgettable men
Three beautiful and *unusual* women**

Come to Whiskey River, Arizona, a place "where
anything can happen. And often does," says
bestselling author JoAnn Ross of her new Temptation
miniseries. "I envision Whiskey River as a romantic,
magical place. A town like Brigadoon, hidden in
the mists, just waiting to be discovered."

Enjoy three very *magical* romances.

#605 *Untamed* (Oct.)

#609 *Wanted!* (Nov.)

#613 *Ambushed* (Dec.)

Come and be spellbound

'Twas the Night Before Christmas...

And all through the inn, not a creature was stirring....
Except college prof Eve Vaughn and the gorgeous, sexy
stranger she'd met. They were sharing the most passionate
night of their lives. It didn't matter that they'd go their
separate ways on Christmas morn. Little did Eve know
madly-in-love Max had *no* intention of letting his special
gift escape!

Enjoy #614 CHRISTMAS WITH EVE by Elda Minger,
available in December 1996.

Five sensuous stories from Temptation about heroes and
heroines who share a single sizzling night of love.... And
damn the consequences!

#615 CHRISTMAS KNIGHT
by Lyn Ellis

Meet Nick De Salvo. Ex-cop. Full-time rebel. To save
a friend, he took the rap for something he didn't do.
Now he's lost his job, but not his instincts. And
intuition tells him that someone wants to see him
brought down. Unfortunately, his only suspect is
T.J. Amberley—the woman who's stolen his heart....

All men are not created equal. Some are rough
around the edges. Tough-minded but tenderhearted.
Incredibly sexy. The tempting fulfillment of every
woman's fantasy.

When it's time to fight for what they believe in, to
win that special woman, our Rebels & Rogues are
heroes at heart.

**Watch for CHRISTMAS KNIGHT
in December 1996, wherever
Harlequin books are sold.**

Mail Order Men—Satisfaction Guaranteed!

Texas Man #5—*Trent Creighton*

This dedicated bachelor is at his wits' end. His three
matchmaking uncles want him to have a woman for
Christmas—and will do anything to see that he gets one!

Rusty Romero can't believe it—her grandmother
actually answered a personal ad for her. What is she?
Desperate? Not that her grandmother has bad taste.
Even Rusty has to admit Trent is drop-dead gorgeous.
But his ideas about women are right out of the Stone
Age. Trent needs a quick lesson in women's lib—and
Rusty knows she's just the woman to give him one.

#616 CHRISTMAS MALE
by Heather MacAllister

Available in December wherever
Harlequin books are sold.

Merry Christmas, Baby!

A romantic collection filled with the magic
of Christmas and the joy of children.

SUSAN WIGGS, Karen Young and
Bobby Hutchinson bring you Christmas wishes,
weddings and romance, in a charming
trio of stories that will warm up your
holiday season.

MERRY CHRISTMAS, BABY! also contains
Harlequin's special gift to you—a set of
FREE GIFT TAGS included in every book.

Brighten up your holiday season with
MERRY CHRISTMAS, BABY!

Available in November at
your favorite retail store.

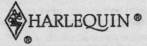

HARLEQUIN ®

◈ HARLEQUIN®

Don't miss these Harlequin favorites by some of our
most distinguished authors! And now you can receive a
discount by ordering two or more titles!

HT#25657	PASSION AND SCANDAL by Candace Schuler	$3.25 U.S $3.75 CAN.	☐ ☐
HP#11787	TO HAVE AND TO HOLD by Sally Wentworth	$3.25 U.S. $3.75 CAN.	☐ ☐
HR#03385	THE SISTER SECRET by Jessica Steele	$2.99 U.S. $3.50 CAN	☐ ☐
HS#70634	CRY UNCLE by Judith Arnold	$3.75 U.S. $4.25 CAN.	☐ ☐
HI#22346	THE DESPERADO by Patricia Rosemoor	$3.50 U.S. $3.99 CAN	☐ ☐
HAR#16610	MERRY CHRISTMAS, MOMMY by Muriel Jensen	$3.50 U.S. $3.99 CAN	☐ ☐
HH#28895	THE WELSHMAN'S WAY by Margaret Moore	$4.50 U.S. $4.99 CAN.	☐ ☐

(limited quantities available on certain titles)

AMOUNT	$
DEDUCT: 10% DISCOUNT FOR 2+ BOOKS	$
POSTAGE & HANDLING	$
($1.00 for one book, 50¢ for each additional)	
APPLICABLE TAXES*	$_____
TOTAL PAYABLE	$_____

(check or money order—please do not send cash)

To order, complete this form and send it, along with a check or money order
for the total above, payable to Harlequin Books, to: **In the U.S.:** 3010 Walden
Avenue, P.O. Box 9047, Buffalo, NY 14269-9047; **In Canada:** P.O. Box 613,
Fort Erie, Ontario, L2A 5X3.

Name: _____

Address: _____ City: _____

State/Prov.: _____ Zip/Postal Code: _____

*New York residents remit applicable sales taxes.
 Canadian residents remit applicable GST and provincial taxes.   HBACK-OD3

Look us up on-line at: http://www.romance.net